AT THE SPEED OF YETI

AT THE SPEED OF YETI

DEMON CODEX™ BOOK 02

LAWRENCE M. SCHOEN
BRIAN THORNE

DISRUPTIVE IMAGINATION

This book is a work of fiction. All of the characters, organizations, and events portrayed in this novel are either products of the author's imagination or are used fictitiously. Sometimes both.

Copyright © 2022 Lawrence M. Schoen and Brian Thorne
Cover by Fantasy Book Design
Cover copyright © LMBPN Publishing

LMBPN Publishing supports the right to free expression and the value of copyright. The purpose of copyright is to encourage writers and artists to produce the creative works that enrich our culture.

The distribution of this book without permission is a theft of the author's intellectual property. If you would like permission to use material from the book (other than for review purposes), please contact support@lmbpn.com. Thank you for your support of the author's rights.

LMBPN Publishing
PMB 196, 2540 South Maryland Pkwy
Las Vegas, NV 89109

Version 1.01, September 2022
ebook ISBN: 979-8-88541-618-4
Print ISBN: 979-8-88541-619-1

*For anyone who has ever climbed the ivory tower,
gazed out at the world from that great height,
and come back down to exit out into the world.*

Adventures await.

THE AT THE SPEED OF YETI TEAM

Thanks to our Beta Team

Rachel Beckford, Larry Omans, Kelly O'Donnell, John Ashmore

Thanks to our JIT Readers
Zacc Pelter
Wendy L Bonell
Peter Manis
Dorothy Lloyd
Paul Westman
Jackey Hankard-Brodie
Deb Mader
Diane L. Smith

If we've missed anyone, please let us know!

Editor
The SkyFyre Editing Team

CHAPTER ONE

Somewhere on the Necromantic Plane

In life, Iosefa Malifa had been many things: visionary, philanthropist, restaurateur, and necromancer. He'd dedicated much of the previous decade to popularizing insects as a food source in an effort to feed the world. As a mage, he'd perfected the near-mythical means of removing the soul from its host body, as well as the more impossible task of putting it back without harm. Immediately prior to his death, he'd simultaneously harnessed the power of three demons from three different planes of existence to shape a combined magic, the like of which hadn't been seen in centuries.

In the end, Malifa, a middle-aged mage from American Samoa—a man of refined tastes and robust appetites whose physical stature had earned him the nickname "Fat Mage"—had died. Amidst unearthly energies, his flesh had dripped from his bones, dissolving into a puddle of ichor. Despite this, his skeleton had survived, transformed in color and substance, forged by arcane forces into a glistening black material that gleamed with a shine reminiscent of obsidian but was actually harder than diamond.

Those shiny dark bones had collapsed into the puddle of his melted flesh but lingered there for only a short while. Some motive force caused them to stir, animate, and reassemble themselves into an upright figure. A greenish glow had lit the skull's empty sockets, suggesting it possessed sight. Even though it lacked lungs to breathe or a tongue to form words, Malifa's voice emanated from that same skull, its jawbone rising and falling in a perfect mockery of the movements of speech. One supposed the skeleton heard sounds, smelled aromas, and felt pressure and pain, warmth and cold—the full range of mortal sensation despite lacking anything like a flesh and blood form.

Malifa had shed his mortality and become something else. He had bid farewell to his oldest and dearest friend, a man he had betrayed in pursuit of an existence beyond mortality. Then, in a new guise as a lich, Malifa had let go of his old pronouns and slipped from the mortal world through a gap into a necromantic realm that was antithetical to life.

The lich felt quite at home there. Free of the concerns and distractions of the flesh, Malifa embraced its transcendence. There were so many new things, so much to learn, and the quietude inherent on that dead plane provided the perfect setting. Like generations of scholars before, Malifa applied its focus to the study of Aoede, the demonic language that had made possible the discovery of most of the other languages, by potentially tapping into the echo of everything that had ever been said aloud. Armed with purpose and focus beyond mortal ken, the lich who had once been a good man of great power began to listen for the pieces that would allow it to transform the world. It knew what shape it intended that world would take.

CHAPTER TWO

Columbo, Sri Lanka

Amidst sweltering heat, in the shade of a third-floor apartment balcony, two women sat across from one another on opposite sides of a small wooden table. The younger woman, a redhead in her twenties, had a look of intense concentration and radiated eagerness. The second woman was blonde, seemingly on the early side of middle age. The raised brows of her expression suggested hesitation and hope. The air between them shimmered. A monkey had leapt from an adjacent tree to the balcony's outer wall, regarded the odd image floating above the table, and fled.

"You don't use a liquid surface?" said the older woman.

"No, ma'am. I—"

"Please, Janice. We'll be spending a lot of time together. Call me Cassandra."

The redhead nodded. "Wijeratne taught me to use the open air. He prefers three-dimensional scrying, and he believes it's more practical."

Cassandra smiled. "Because there's never a bowl of water when you need it?"

Janice blushed. "He's very pragmatic that way."

"I appreciate that. It's part of why I'm here. He's spoken very highly of you. There are precious few Everett speakers in the world, and fewer still of substantial power. Wijeratne believes you have power but insufficient training. He's asked me to take you on and train you as I once trained him."

"You trained him?"

"I did."

"But Wijeratne is in his fifties, and you're..."

Cassandra smiled again. "Older than I appear. Evidence that a proper diet can make a real difference. That is a good segue for us to begin on."

"It is?"

"An Everett practitioner typically perceives parallel realities up and down the recent timeline. With sufficient power, the language can be used to look back much further. As we gaze deeper into the past, events quickly become fixed. History is infinitely less volatile but still informative. To appreciate this, you need to understand where we began. I'll guide you to a series of moments, but it will be your words, your power, which allows us to witness each time and place."

England, 1588

Despite being the bastard son of Sir Edward Dyer, the particulars of Edward Thomas' illegitimacy caused him no upset. His father had ensured that he received the best of opportunities and education, and the younger Edward grew up on the fringes of court. Like his father before him, Thomas had been tutored by no less remarkable a mind than the brilliant mathematician and astrologer John Dee. It was thus, with a great appreciation of irony, that he found himself standing in John Dee's home while that worthy individual was away in Poland.

It should be noted that Edward Thomas was not in Dee's

house by invitation but had come at the behest of two other men on the off chance they needed a plausible excuse for being there. Thomas could claim an association with Dee and was thus a plausible visitor. His two companions bore Dee only ill will, and Edward had regretted bringing them to the house from the moment they'd arrived.

All three men were part of a larger group. They called themselves the *Disciples*. Self-appointed men of action, they anonymously corrected what they perceived to be the impieties of others who possessed both power and status. Such individuals might otherwise go free of social corrections were it not for the activities of the Disciples. Edward's involvement in the group was still probationary; several members admired his quick mind and had vouchsafed his religious rigor.

Others had expressed concern that because he had been a student of Dee's, that same quick mind might be filled with thoughts of alchemy, witchcraft, and illicit communications with angels and demons. This current mission, under the supervision of two senior members of the group, was a test of Edward's commitment to the cause.

The three men breached the house with ease. Dee had gone to Poland with occultist Edward Kelley and fellow alchemist Albert Łaski some years before, leaving behind a pair of aging staff as caretakers. Those two were easily overpowered and temporarily locked in a pantry. The plan included setting them free later so they could spread the word of the Disciples' visit.

The specifics would eventually find their way back to Dee. After all, what good was a punishment if the offender went unaware of its infliction? With that in mind, the three men protected their identities by wearing theatrical masks and referring to one another by the names of saints. Edward Thomas had been designated "St. Andrew."

The purpose of the visit was not simple robbery; they were, it should be remembered, gentlemen. After securing the servants, they did consider ransacking the home, but instead, they headed to its sizable library, arguably the greatest in England. Dee had originally proposed a national library to Queen Elizabeth, and when Her Majesty declined, he had kept the collection he had gathered and continued adding to it. There, in more volumes than any God-fearing man could conceive of, the Disciples expected to find proof of Dee's impieties. At the moment, though, the sheer quantity of books dwarfed the men's capacity. While all three had been college-educated, only St. Andrew possessed the intellect and wit to comprehend the volumes written in Dee's own hand. Volumes his fellow saints believed contained unwitting confessions of the alchemist's transgressions.

"I understood it was a large collection," St. Peter muttered. He was standing on the library's threshold, trying to take it all in. "But I had…no idea."

"We are committed," insisted St. Paul. "Committed by burglary and assault if simple moral conviction is insufficient to your needs. While we might lack the time or perspicacity to lay our hands upon proof of Dee's misdeeds, we can still send a message. With luck and the blessings of the Almighty, that might be sufficient to save Dee's soul and return him to the path of righteousness."

"What form is that message to take?" asked St. Andrew.

"Cleansing fire," replied St. Paul. "I propose we burn them all."

St. Andrew balked, and St. Peter looked stunned, though a moment later the man nodded in agreement.

"What, all of them?"

"Every last volume," insisted St. Paul. His eyes were alight with piety.

St. Andrew gazed around the room. The greatest collection in England was before him. His compatriots, educated men both, were prepared to transform it to ash, and there was nothing he could do to stop them. If he refused to assist or tried to prevent them, he had no doubt that he would be ejected from the Disciples. Paul and Peter would simply return without him on another day and do the job by themselves. Choosing not to participate would not save a single book, and he did not relish the thought of how the Disciples might respond to his perceived betrayal.

"We must take care so the message is not misunderstood."

"How do you mean?" asked St. Peter.

"We must contain the fire to this room, damaging no other portion of the house, so our intention is clear. Dee must understand that it was his books, his vessels of sin, which brought down our wrath."

Paul smiled at him. "An excellent consideration. Let us be about it."

He and Peter had discussed this intention before sharing the plan with St. Andrew and had come prepared with the necessary materials. St. Andrew made use of various rugs and tapestries, rolling them up tight and drenching them with water he brought from the well. These he positioned to block the spread of fire to the rest of the house.

"Set it ablaze," instructed St. Paul. His command was directed at St. Andrew. This was his test—that the destruction would proceed by his hand. Should the matter ever come before the courts, by virtue of that distinction and the high births of his companions (and his own position as a bastard), all blame and all consequence would land on him. Nonetheless, screaming inside at the senseless but inevitable waste, he took tinderbox in hand and with a single strike, set the room to burn.

"Let us adjourn to the hallway," suggested St. Peter. "We can linger there long enough to ensure the library is well on its way to complete consumption and the fire does not cross the threshold and expand into the rest of the house."

"Indeed," agreed St Paul. "We do not wish to endanger the staff."

They did that, and only then did St. Andrew notice that Paul had rescued a decanter of brandy from a library table. They stood outside in the hall looking in, passing the liquor among themselves, and watched as Dee's books and shelves burned. When St. Paul was satisfied that things were proceeding as desired, the three men returned to the pantry where they had left the house's retainers trussed up like a pair of elderly geese. St. Andrew loosened their bonds and informed them that the library was burning but the fire would, in all probability, spare the rest of the house. Such assurances did little to quell the fear in the servants' eyes, and when it was clear the trio had no other plans for them, they fled.

"It would be well if we were to follow their example," St. Andrew murmured, the image of the burning library occupying his mind's eye. The loss was already weighing on his soul. He followed the other two out into the night. They walked for the better part of an hour, removing their masks as they entered more populated surroundings. Then, at the appointed location, each went his own way.

If all followed according to plan, the full complement of Disciples would meet at their usual place, the private room of a popular Oxford tavern, in a fortnight's time. Committed by his actions, Edward Thomas had every intention of attending that meeting. Before that—indeed, the very next night—he surreptitiously went back to Dee's home. The staff had not yet returned, and by lamplight he moved through the building until he reached the library. He could not say what drove him there. Guilt at what he'd done? The need to see proof of his actions and the full consequences of his questionable judgment? Or perhaps, just perhaps, the faint hope that something might have been spared. It was this last that proved to be the case. Of the entire contents of the library, a single shelf held a few unharmed books. As he handled them, he saw they were not merely unburned but unblemished. The surrounding ash fell away from them as if he had brushed them with a feather duster, leaving the books untouched and pristine.

He gathered them in his arms, though there were almost too many to carry, and took them away with him. He left ashen footprints throughout the rest of the house and out onto the road as he returned to the simple cottage his father had arranged for him on his Aunt Mary's estate.

He pored over the untouched books for the rest of the night and into the next day, trying to understand what he had saved. One book, a slim volume that was little more than a bound leaflet, explained why these had been spared in the fire. It detailed the methods for preserving books that John Dee had proposed to the queen when he'd recommended the national library, methods never before seen in England that drew on his research in alchemy. The books were indestructible, and each was irreplaceable.

The remainder of the volumes save one consisted of philosophical arguments and alchemical treatises. Some of the ideas were daring, others shocking, but none would upset a bishop or justify the actions of the Disciples. Edward Thomas had no doubt that if he were ever questioned, they would insist the incriminating works had been consumed by the fire.

The last book, though, the largest of the lot, provided all the motivation needed for burning the library to ash. Any member of the clergy could see that it contained page after page of heresy. It was a treatise on divine treason. Dee was known to have spent years of his life seeking to speak with angels. It was likewise believed that he had mastered a modicum of their Enochian language.

This last and fattest book showed that he had done far more. Its dozens of sections were transcriptions rendered in the Roman alphabet, written in a flowing hand, each in a different language not spoken in the world. From what Edward could glean as he studied the cramped notes scribbled in the margins in English, each section presented a series of rituals and invocations that made it possible to converse with higher beings from other realms.

Edward Thomas stared at this last volume until his candle sputtered out. He took it to bed with him as if to protect it despite its immunity to fire. He clasped the volume tightly with both arms and fell asleep making his plans for the next day. If Dee was a madman, the contents of the book were merely his ravings, and possession of it, while still heresy, would harm no one. If any part of it was true, it represented a power never before matched on Earth.

The next morning, taking his inspiration from his fellow—and now former—Disciples, he set fire to his cottage. Officially, Edward Thomas died in that fire. St. Andrew, meanwhile, left England. His ultimate destination was the home of his best friend from school, a fellow who now made his home in the tiny nation of San Marino. That simple decision would change the world.

CHAPTER THREE

Alexander University, Philadelphia
Alberto "Albert" Hernandez Alcaldo occupied the only open space in the former broom closet that functioned as his office. He had long since accepted that the crowded nature of the tiny room was a problem of his own making.

The office was filled from floor to ceiling with the accouterments, both arcane and mundane, required of any aspiring magic user. Books were stacked on every shelf, on his desk, on the table he had had to disassemble to get through the door, on nearly every bit of the floor, and on top of other books, tomes, and palimpsests, creating unsteady towers of paper that threatened to topple at the slightest provocation. Their titles ranged from indecipherable, archaic runes that served as a shibboleth to keep lesser students away to the best-selling *Necromancy 101: Raising the Dead for Fun and Profit*.

A narrow desk pinned against one wall was the largest piece of furniture, but a casual observer would have been hard-pressed to identify it beneath the books and multicolored sticky notes. Pens and highlighters whose colors spanned the rainbow stood sentinel in ceramic coffee cups of a dozen different shapes and slogans. A brand-new and very expensive Mac laptop enjoyed prime real estate at the center of the desk.

What drew the eye more than anything else in the tiny office was the lavish hamster habitat. It occupied the right end of Albert's desk in all its garish neon glory, rising ever higher via multiple ribbed tubes that granted access to a gleaming plastic suite of rooms as well as an attached penthouse apartment replete with wood shavings and a miniature Pottery Barn-esque chaise longue.

The only portion of the floor not stacked with books or furniture was a small space Albert had covered in arcane sigils organized in a perfectly executed ring. Mirror images of that summoning circle shone on his dual computer monitors in high-definition, painstaking geometric precision.

Albert stood next to the circle, the toes of his Tom Ford driving moccasins almost brushing it in the cramped confines. The overhead light had been turned off, but his Mediterranean features and rich black hair glowed in the light of a scintillating ball of sapphire-tinged fire that hovered in the space above the sigils, occupying the exact center of the room.

On the desk, Albert's imp familiar, H.H., sat on its furry hamster haunches and removed a tiny pair of sunglasses from its left cheek pouch. It slid them onto its face before its disconcertingly deep voice rang out in encouragement.

"You've got this, Albert, trust me. You're drawing on a significant amount of magical energy and from the elemental 'ry realm, no less. This is by far the most magic you've handled since coming off your medications. Congratulations, you've got the juice."

"Thanks," the grad student rasped, his voice shaky and strained. After years of reliance on his meds, reducing and eventually eliminating them had brought wild mood swings and left him physically wrung out. Through it all, he had clung to the promise of his goal. Daily, he had told himself that gaining access to his Will would be worth any price.

But the hell hamster wasn't done. "Without focus, you're a danger to yourself and everyone around you. You need to channel your Will and bend that power into your spell."

Albert grunted. "Being able to focus was why I was taking those ADHD meds!"

"Being on those drugs was why you couldn't tap into your Will."

The ball of fire intensified. Orange and blue flames pushed outward as it expanded and filled the room. Nearby papers began to curl at their edges.

Sweat beaded on Albert's temples and trickled down his face. His lips flickered with the movements of the 'ry tongue—the language of the Realm of Flame—and the syllables rasped from his throat.

Albert's hands drifted in front of him as if borne up by the heat, moving in time with the pulsing flames. He brought his chin up and raised his voice as the energy built beyond his ability to control it and threatened to free itself from the summoning circle.

Then, with a surge of Will, Albert brought his hands together in a thunderous clap.

The ball of elemental flame shrank as if chastised, and its exterior acquired a solid, glistening shell. Its newly hardened surface cracked and transformed, and five pieces of burned crystal clattered to the floor at the young mage's feet.

A moment passed. Albert stopped speaking. He wiped the sweat from his brow, then knelt in his skinny jeans to inspect his work.

The stones, black gems shot through with red streaks, gleamed with an inner light. They were beautiful and unlike anything that naturally occurred in the world. Then they started to move.

Albert sucked in a breath and rose. From its perch on the desk, H.H. looked down.

"You're gonna want to pick those up, but make sure you use an oven mitt."

Albert looked at the imp. "Why?"

H.H. simply pointed at the floor. The gems first writhed, then hopped and bounced on the old wood. As they moved, they began to elongate. Their shapes warped and stretched until Albert was staring at five red and black lizards, each about three inches in length.

"Salamanders," he whispered in awe. "It worked. I conjured salamanders."

A combination of the cramped space and his amazement caused Albert to slide a foot across the summoning circle, breaking the protection of its seal. The elementals scurried free, and Albert's awe turned to panic.

The tiny creatures spurted gouts of flame from their lipless mouths as they scurried about the office, setting books and papers ablaze.

"Dammit!" The mage lunged and scooped up one of the diminutive demons.

The salamander's stony flesh blistered his fingers on contact, forcing him to drop it. *"¡Dios!"*

"I told you...oven mitts." H.H. shook its head before leaping off the desk.

Sucking on his wounded fingers, Albert reached for the door with his other hand and opened it just wide enough to thrust his arm out. He felt about for a moment before grabbing a fire extinguisher mounted on the outer wall and yanking it back in the room, then slammed the door before any of the salamanders could escape.

The imp dashed across the floor after the demons. "Look, Albert, I'm in hot pursuit! Ha! See what I did there?"

Albert groaned as he pulled the pin to activate the extinguisher.

H.H. caught up to its prey and scooped the first salamander into its mouth, disregarding the elemental's size. Its cheeks bulged.

The mage depressed the lever on the extinguisher, and the remaining salamanders squealed, lost from sight amidst the blast.

A moment passed. All Albert could hear was the skittering of tiny legs and an occasional squeal of protest in the fog.

Finally, the office was silent.

Albert waved his hand to clear the air in front of his face. "Is it safe to open the door?"

"Yep," came the imp's muffled reply.

Albert turned the knob and stepped into the empty foyer of the school's Department of Demonic Languages. The secretary's desk was unoccupied, as usual.

He sighed in relief as he swung the door back and forth to create a draft.

H.H. emerged, raised a paw to its mouth to shove a stony black tail that was attempting to escape back inside, and stood on hind legs to face its mage.

"You got all of them?" asked Albert.

The imp adjusted its cheeks, manually reducing them to normal size before replying. "Yep. All five. They're squirmy little bastards."

Albert didn't care. With the crisis averted, his sense of elation crept back in, a welcome contrast to the sense of helpless despair that had visited him since ending his meds.

"Holy shit! I did it."

H.H. looked up at him with all the disdain a hamster's face could muster. "What you did was almost burn down your office and risk setting the whole building on fire, or worse, if these guys had gotten loose,"

Albert waved the objection away. "You had me covered. We both know that."

"Well, yeah, but..."

"But nothing. I mustered enough Will to draw together salamanders. *Five* of them. That's...that's crazy. That's, like, in the top three percent of 'ry users. *I* did that."

"Well, yeah," repeated H.H. "You've got a real talent for those nasal vowels. Did your professor teach you that?"

The grad student nodded. "I've been practicing for years. My pronunciation has always been good, but I never had any Will to back it up. I had the concentration. I had the skill, but until now, I never had the power."

"I'm going to skip the obvious He-Man reference," remarked H.H. "We suspected your lack of oomph was because of your meds. This just proves it. Sure, withdrawal has been tough, but you're through the worst of it. So, now that you can *fire things up*, what are you going to do?"

Albert ignored the imp's pun. He set the extinguisher back in its cradle and left a note for the secretary that it needed to be refilled. Then, returning to his office, he grabbed a rag and some solvent from atop a bookshelf and began wiping the sigils off the floor. "I don't know. It's a lot to think about. I've barely been able to muster any Will before. I guess I'd gotten used to what I *couldn't* do and adjusted my plans accordingly. This changes the whole paradigm."

"I bet." H.H. snorted. "Funny, those meds would probably come in real handy right now as you try to think about what to do next."

As the last of the sigils vanished, Albert considered his familiar's remark before shaking his head. "No. I'm never going back. The meds aren't an option," he insisted. "But maybe a conversation with the person who suggested I go off them would help."

"You want to talk with Dani?"

"I think it makes sense. You don't agree?"

The hamster took the rag from Albert's hand before he stood up, folded it neatly, and scrambled across the furniture to place it in a cubby. "Maybe, though I think your first visit should be with the psychiatrist who prescribed the meds. Maybe have him do a full workup. Ya know, in case we missed something. Sometimes stopping psych drugs can be as bad as taking them."

Albert frowned at the imp. "We both know how that would end. Dr. Doyle doesn't trust magic, and he certainly doesn't understand it."

"Fine. Then I guess we'll go back to the puppy farm. Ugh."

"What? You liked the puppies."

"No. I liked them when they were singing, gyrating Elvi. In that form, they were fabulous. As puppies, they're just…messy."

CHAPTER FOUR

Columbo, Sri Lanka

It was the same balcony but a different day. The previous scrying effort had not merely exhausted Janice but had produced a migraine that left her incapacitated for forty-eight hours. Once again, she sat across from Cassandra, but the eagerness of the previous meeting had been replaced by reluctance and a hint of dread.

"You're scared." It was all statement, no part question.

Janice squirmed. "Using Everett has never been painful before."

"Examining the past, especially years that predate our own existence, is unnatural. Your brain has never experienced anything like it. Doing so also broadens your reach when you look at parallels to the current moment, which is how you'll mainly use the language."

"This was how you trained Wijeratne? By gazing into the past?"

"It was. It was painful and difficult for him as well. I promise you, it does get easier. I selected this next scrying so that you will understand how the distant past affects magic users to this very day. Now, summon your Will, and I will guide you through it."

As it had days before, a region of air the size of a basketball began to shimmer between them. Moments later, the past unfolded.

San Marino, 1631

Brother Marinus—the latest in the long line of monks named after Saint Marinus, the founder of the city—stood atop the ramparts of Montale. His thick black hair and beard rippled in the breeze as he gazed down the rocky slopes of Monte Titano. Below him, dozens of armed horsemen snaked their way up the winding road from the valley floor. "So, they have finally come."

Next to him, an adolescent novitiate named Antonius looked up quizzically. "Who are they?"

"*Malatesta*," Marinus spat. "Or rather, those dogs are all that is left of House Malatesta. Once they were a powerful family, but now they work as mercenaries under their *condottieri* Pandolfo, an ignorant and brutal man. They are no better than thieves arriving at the cusp of night, but they cloak themselves in the legitimacy of their employers."

"Mercenaries? Why would such men attack us? Who paid them to besiege us? And why? We are simple monks." Antonius' bewilderment was written on his face.

"You are young and full of faith. I hesitate to burden you with the truth. These mongrels have come at the behest of Rome."

"The Church? Surely not!"

Marinus turned his stony gaze away from the approaching Malatesta and studied the novitiate's face, weighing how much to tell him. "We have welcomed the persecuted to San Marino for centuries. We have housed them, educated them, and protected them. All of this you know, but did you never imagine that someday the persecutors might follow? You have much to learn, Antonius.

"I had imagined having the luxury of time for your instruction, but the situation has changed. The next phase of your education must begin now. There is no time to argue. Run and seek out Brother Paolo. When you find him, escort him to the vaults. Immediately!"

Antonius was confused, but he was also disciplined. He nodded once to indicate his understanding and acquiescence, then took off at a sprint, his bare feet flying down the steps to the courtyard.

Marinus watched him go, praying that sufficient time remained. He took one last look down the mountain. As the last light of day left the valley floor, he saw the unmistakable red and yellow checks of the Malatestan colors streaming from a ragged banner at the front of the column.

"Come along then, Pandolfo. I will give you a message to take back to Rome."

Antonius found Paolo in the main library, asleep at a desk. He gently roused the ancient monk and led him by the hand out of the room. The blind brother knew his way around the tower citadel, though his pace was slower than a crippled donkey. The novitiate tried to make haste, but Paolo shrugged off his arm and would not be rushed. He tottered along and distracted the novitiate from hurrying by interrogating him.

"Tell me again what you saw, Antonius. Speak plainly but leave nothing out."

The young man sighed. "Armed men on horses. Many of them."

Paolo interrupted. "Be more specific, lad. How many men? What did they carry? What were their colors?"

Antonius had finally gotten them to a flight of stone stairs that wrapped around the inside wall of *Montale*. This time Brother Paolo accepted the lad's assistance as they navigated downward. Antonius sighed with relief as he began easing his elderly companion down one step after another. "Thirty, maybe forty men. I didn't see their colors, but Marinus told me they were led by someone named Pandolfo."

Paolo rolled his sightless eyes. "That makes sense. That man was never bothered by ethics. He just wants money. Money and his so-called glory. What else?"

"They were all on horseback. I think I saw some muskets."

"Hmmm. What about a wagon? Did you see a wagon?"

Antonius stopped. "I don't remember. Does it matter?"

"Would I ask if it didn't matter? Try harder, Antonius. We live in a converted prison. Muskets can't hurt us, but a cannon most surely will, and for that, they would need wagons."

"What do they want from us, Brother Paolo?"

"Knowledge, Antonius. They want to steal our knowledge."

"Why?"

"Because knowledge brings power, and they would take ours for their own."

Pandolfo Malatesta sat high in the saddle and gazed up at the candle-lit windows of Montale, the tower on the shortest of San Marino's three peaks. His men had formed a perimeter around the only entrance to the former prison—a single door set more than a man's height above the ground.

A moment later, his youngest brother Pietro approached with the news he had waited to hear.

"The gun is assembled, *Condottiere*. Shall we give them a chance to surrender?"

Pandolfo slipped a hand inside his jacket to finger the

contract he kept safely tucked away but always near. The paper promised his family a return of their lands and titles. It promised him the chance to correct years of shame and abuse by men who, by all rights, should have been licking his boots. So many wrongs would be redressed, but only if he retrieved the book Rome so desperately wanted—the book of black magic the heathens inside had kept hidden for so long.

"No, Pietro. They know we're here, and they know why we've come. They've had many years and many opportunities to do what is right. Tonight, they will pay the price for their crimes against God."

Pietro knew better than to argue. He turned on his heel and hurried back to issue orders to the trio of men who manned the cannon.

"Prepare to fire!"

CHAPTER FIVE

<u>Alexander University, Philadelphia</u>
Professor Derrick Watson, a leading expert in the field of demonic languages, tugged his hair as he paced his office. He was dressed in khaki slacks and an untucked flannel shirt. As any of his students would have reported, he'd never cared about fashion, but even by his own lax academic standards, he looked rumpled.

His office fared little better than his wardrobe. It was spacious and comfortable but decorated grudgingly. A large wooden desk occupied its center, and two not-quite-matching guest chairs faced it. A mishmash of bookshelves lined every inch of the room. Against the wall and alongside the entrance, a battered but serviceable sofa held the form of Miss Patricia "Trixie" Gallagher. She wore blue jeans and a teal Alexander University hoodie against the fall weather.

Trixie was an extremely talented undergraduate majoring in alchemy. She had graduated from high school early, worked for some time as a pharmacy tech, and then spent two years accompanying Doctors Without Borders through war zones, drought, and famine, helping administer much-needed medications to refugees around the globe.

Her parents, deeply religious Irish-Catholics who owned a small drug store in Baltimore, had tried to discourage her. They'd failed but rejoiced when, upon her return to the US, she'd announced her intention to return to school. She had entered the university with an accelerated program of study. At present, she was a senior and was enrolled in every honors program the institution offered. Her coursework and her remarks in class routinely impressed her peers and her professors alike. She also volunteered at a women's crisis line and had helped manage three food drives. In her remaining time, she was dating Professor Watson.

Pacing wasn't helping the professor. If anything, Watson had grown more agitated. He had progressed from simple steps to actively stomping around the room, a clear reflection of his souring mood. Several times, he had pulled books off the shelves, a gleam of hope shining in his eyes as he selected each volume. He required only a few moments of flipping pages and glancing at particulars before discarding each, the first with a *whuff* of disgust and the last with an outright snarl. More stomping followed as he crossed the small room to assault a different bookshelf. At some level, he knew it was all theatrics. The problem didn't lie with the books. It was him, or rather, the cacophony of unwanted thoughts that kept intruding on his concentration. He'd lost his focus, and the distraction couldn't have happened at a worse time.

"This sabbatical is bullshit," he muttered as he slammed another book back onto its shelf. "What was Dean Templeton thinking? How can we locate any fragments of the *Demon Codex* if I can't do my research? How am I supposed to do this alone?"

Trixie crossed her legs on the couch and tapped her foot impatiently. She held her tongue and instead gathered her long hair and pulled it into a ponytail, her only commentary a quiet sigh. Derrick had been through a lot recently. They all had, but him especially. Being betrayed by your closest friend and witnessing his multiple attacks against current and former students would stress anyone out. Since his meeting with the dean, his behavior had grown more pointless and wholly unproductive.

Trixie hated it when things stopped being productive. More, it was agonizing to watch him in such a state, and her silence wasn't helping.

"Derrick, you're losing it. Come sit with me for a moment and compose your thoughts." She patted the leather cushion next to her.

Watson stopped stomping. A sheepish look crept onto his face, and he let the latest book slip from his grasp and onto the desk as he crossed to the sofa. He sat as instructed, took a deep breath, and ran his hands over his face before speaking.

"Malifa told us...told *me*...what he was going to do next. He's tracking down other pieces of the *Demon Codex*, and he intends to match them with past students of mine who have demonstrated expertise in those languages."

The act of summarizing the situation out loud, falling into "lecture mode," relaxed him. His shoulders dipped as some of the tension drained out of him and the distraction faded from his eyes.

Trixie held his hand comfortingly as he settled into his thoughts. "You mentioned Albert had pulled in contact details through a friend in the alumni office. Once you've sorted through them, you'll be able to phone or email the most likely prospects to warn them."

"But that's just it. I'm not sure where to start. There are dozens, maybe hundreds of potential targets if I include undergrads who took advanced courses in one or more languages. What if I delay contacting my best former grad student in 'ry to focus on another who speaks Euskal? Worse still, what if warning them is what Malifa wants me to do?"

Trixie slipped both of her hands around his arm and drew

herself closer to him. She leaned over and kissed his cheek. "You're overthinking this."

"Am I? We've already seen that he understands how my mind works. He and I have known each other since we were roommates in college, and across all those years, when we played chess together, he beat me nine games out of ten. He always claimed it wasn't just that he could see more moves ahead but also he could predict what I was planning. Now, after everything that's just happened... Frankly, he's in my head, and I don't know what to believe. I'd thought I was making my own decisions, my own choices. It turns out he's been calling the shots and staying three steps ahead all along. He's used our friendship to manipulate me at every turn."

Trixie kissed him again, then pulled back, her eyes twinkling in the office's light. "My dad told me that when he was in the Army, they were taught how to respond to being ambushed. They were taught that inaction was what got people killed. Doing something made the other guy react, and that could buy you time or opportunity. Do something unexpected, something he can't predict, and then, you know, build from that. Your life isn't a two-dimensional chess game. I don't care how well he thinks he knows you, Derrick Watson; he doesn't know your heart. A man like him never could."

Watson's jaw dropped. "You're right. That's it! That's how we can beat him. With the unexpected!"

She responded with a broad smile, but it was short-lived. The professor took her hands in his and slipped off the couch, then dropped to one knee with a hopeful expression plastered across his face.

"I-I love you, Trixie. My feelings for you aren't a crush or an infatuation or a midlife crisis. Malifa putting you in danger made me realize that. Made me realize I didn't care about living without you. I'm telling you this, not just because it's the most unexpected thing I might do, but because it's true, and I'm finally admitting it to myself. I love you. And, well, I... Patricia Margaret Gallagher, will you marry me?"

Trixie's reaction was abrupt and physical. She shoved him, both hands striking his chest and tumbling him onto his ass. As he sprawled on the office floor, she jumped to her feet. A primal growl escaped her lips. "Marry you? Are you out of your fucking mind? Oh. My. *God!*"

The young woman took over stomping about the office. Watson remained frozen in his spot on the floor while Trixie tore a path back and forth and expounded upon the errors of his ways.

"First off, I'm only twenty-one. This isn't the freaking Dark Ages anymore. You know, the seventies? I haven't even graduated college. I haven't started my doctorate yet. I have stuff to do. Damnit, Derrick, I don't even know if I *believe* in marriage."

Watson opened his mouth to reply but thought better of it.

"Second, my parents would lose their shit! My dad's a veteran, Derrick, and I don't want him to kill me or you because you're in some sort of crisis, midlife or otherwise. I mean, what the hell? Do you feel the need to lock me up? Are you that insecure about our relationship? Do you think a piece of paper will fix that? Come on!"

Trixie continued to lecture, and Watson wisely continued to pretend he didn't exist.

"And you want to do this *now*? In the middle of the Malifa crisis? Seriously? A necromancer turned himself into an immortal lich, and he's seeking even more power so he can do whatever he wants to the world. He already possessed the minds of two of your past students. He almost killed both of us, and he did that with only a couple sections of the *Demon Codex*. Now he's after the whole damn thing. You..." She pointed a finger at Watson. "God help us, *you* might be the only person who can stop him, and you want to get *married*? Arggghhh! Do you even remember his parting words? Do you?"

"He promised he'd come for more of my students."

"Exactly."

Watson was not an idiot, and he knew an opening when he saw one.

"Okay. Okay. You're right. My timing is terrible. I need your help to plan a way ahead and quickly. If we're going to figure out who to reach first, I need you to help me do the research and prioritize. Otherwise, Malifa...the lich, wins."

"I know that!"

Derrick patted the air with his hands and slowly stood up to face the woman he loved, albeit from a safe distance.

"The thing is, even if he were to track down more of my past students, it won't do him any good."

"Right," agreed Trixie. "He'd need to have more pages from the book, the pieces to allow those students to summon demons from the realms they have their language expertise in."

"Which gives us two prongs of attack. Reach out to those former students..."

"...and try to track down the remaining portions of the *Demon Codex*, but how? Until Malifa began finding them, they'd all been lost for centuries."

"Not all," replied Derrick. "I-I might have overstated the case before. I suspect that a former student of mine in China knows where one can be found, and I know for a fact that one of the pieces is in Iceland."

"Iceland? How do you know that? Why there?"

"The Aurora."

"The what?"

"The Aurora Borealis. The Northern Lights. The individual guarding that portion of *gli Anderlibri* has an...affinity for the Northern Lights. He likes them."

"Wait, so you've known about someone who's had one of these books all along, and you didn't do anything yet? You aren't worried he's going to summon a demon?"

"Don't get too caught up on the D-word. A 'demon' is just a sapient being from another realm. Someone tied to the language and thus the magic of that place. To any of them, if you showed up in their realm, you'd be seen as a demon too."

Trixie crossed her arms. "Thanks for repeating the lecture from your 101 class. I really needed it."

"Sorry."

"Fine, but haven't you worried that he might use the book to bring over one of those demons?"

"Nope. Not a chance."

"Why not?"

"Because he's made it his mission to use the fragment to make sure no one else taps into the magic of that particular realm."

"That doesn't make much sense. Why would he do that?"

"Enlightened self-interest. Also, he's the most fluent speaker of that language on Earth."

"Wouldn't that make it even more dangerous for him to have that piece of the book?"

Watson shook his head. "Not in this case. He's fluent because he's a native speaker. Because it's his realm. He's a demon."

"A demon?"

"Only technically. More specifically, he's a yeti."

CHAPTER SIX

Puppies of Healing Farm

Albert ran his hands over the comfy upholstery of the oversized armchair as he settled in place. American decor rarely appealed to him, but the farmhouse thing had grown on him during his visits.

H.H. was less comfortable.

The imp perched atop the back of the same chair and glared at a gaggle of puppies that had gathered at Albert's feet. They ignored Albert, preferring to stare up at H.H., their eyes full of unspoken canine hopes. The imp glared back.

"They want to eat me."

Albert chuckled. "No. They want to play with you. They might chew on you a bit, but other than roughhousing, I doubt they'd know what to do with you if they caught you."

"Why do they all look funny? Dogs in commercials always look the same."

"You're thinking of pure breeds. These are mutts. Dani only uses puppies that have been rescued from shelters or otherwise abandoned. She gives them new homes and a family."

"They still look funny."

Before Albert could further explain, Dr. Danielle "Dani" Leroux came in from the kitchen carrying a tray piled high with coffee and beignets. She'd grown up in a family of cooks in New Orleans, and Albert salivated like Pavlov's own dog every time she served her heavenly pastries.

She was followed by her new boyfriend, FBI agent Stanley Chen, carrying an assortment of cups and plates. Dani put the service on the coffee table and sat on the couch opposite Albert. Stanley took the place alongside her and began dishing out beverages and carbs.

After everyone had been served, Dani leaned forward.

"Based on everything you've told us, it sounds like you've had more than sufficient Will all along. It never manifested—and you never realized your potential—because you started taking the ADHD medication long before you learned anything that would allow you to tap into your natural power. That doesn't mean the work you've done with Professor Watson over the last few years has been a waste. It's understandable if you've entertained such thoughts, but that's just an artifact of withdrawal."

"So, all that work. It wasn't in vain?"

"Just the opposite. If anything, the meds facilitated your focus, and you've probably acquired more than his other students could have over the same time. He's repeatedly bragged about your linguistic proficiency. You do realize he considers you the best grad student he's ever had, don't you?"

Albert blushed. "It doesn't feel like it."

Dani shrugged, uncertain if his modesty was due to low self-esteem or if he didn't believe her assessment of his newly accessible abilities. Since she couldn't do anything about the former, she focused on the latter. "Think of it like this. Someone set up a bank account in your name. You didn't know the account existed, let alone that it was receiving regular deposits every month. Now, suddenly, all the money that's built up is yours to spend."

Stanley chimed in, "And not only has it been accruing interest, it's like you've been taking classes and picking up advanced degrees in business finance and marketing. You don't just have access to the cash. You have the knowledge of how best to use it."

Dani shook her head. "Mmm, yes and no. On the one hand, the meds have kept Albert focused even as they cut him off from his Will, and while going off the meds means gaining access to his Will, it also means losing control over that focus. In some respects, it doesn't matter how much skill or knowledge he has if a lack of attention means it never occurs to him to change gears and tap into a different portion of what he knows."

Albert nodded. "The professor has always insisted that command of the language at hand is critical to any magic."

"He tells all his grad students that," agreed Dani.

Stanley smiled in agreement. "And he follows it up by noting that understanding the language is only the entry-level of magical access. True mastery comes from creating complex utterances that allow for greater effects."

"That's the difference, in a nutshell, between ordinary practitioners and full-blown mages," explained Dani.

"Assuming you have the Will and can control the magical forces involved. That takes practice," Stanley added.

"Right."

Dani tapped a finger against her lips. "Maybe I'm biased as a scientist, but I've always felt that magic is like chemistry. The language provides the building blocks, much like the elements of the periodic chart. Mastery comes from combining individual elements into molecules that are something entirely new with different attributes and capabilities."

H.H. snorted and muttered, "Humans. You overcomplicate everything."

Albert ignored his familiar and responded to Dani. "Even if what you say is correct, it isn't enough. If it was, Will wouldn't matter. Control wouldn't matter."

Stanley jumped on board. "I agree. Maybe the difference

between ordinary practitioners and full mages is more like theater. Every playwright has access to the same words, but few will produce a masterpiece. Basically, once you compose and master a spell, it becomes a thing unto itself, not simply a collection of words. Metaphorically, it's a solid and solitary unit, possessing both intention and purpose."

Dani reached over and took Stanley's hand. "I like that. It captures the skill and dedication required while leaving room for the art, the intangible piece that separates a great magic user from a mundane cantrip-caster. Unlike writing, magic requires you to be both the playwright and the actor."

"Exactly. That's how my time-reversal spell works."

Albert looked at Stanley with renewed interest. "How do you mean?"

"When I first came up with the spell, it only rolled time back for a little less than a minute. It was difficult and complex by most people's standards, but the results were still fairly minor. That's usually the case when working in Maxwell. It wasn't until I worked out how to use the spell to buy myself an extra minute during the casting that I was able to extend its duration."

"Like building blocks."

"Exactly. Every time I cast it, I add a block to the structure of the spell to the point where nowadays, if there is enough sauce—"

Albert interrupted him, shaking his head in confusion. "Sauce?"

"Sorry, that's a slang term some of us use for magical energy. Some say 'aether' or 'mojo.' Whatever the term, it's the stuff that slips from another realm into our world at a given point in time and makes that type of magic possible. Anyway, if I have enough available, I can extend the time-reversal to over fifteen minutes before it becomes too unwieldy."

"Wow, that's a lot of sauce." Albert rolled that idea around in his head, then asked, "What are the mechanics of that?"

"Obviously, part of it is the language. I've rehearsed the

cadence and pronunciation so extensively that it requires no concentration on my part. Frankly, anyone with fluency in Maxwell could manage that, but the transitions between the building blocks require experience, exceptional timing, and Will. I have to invest power into the spell to join the blocks. Each block adds to the burden. I have to keep the manipulated energy in a balanced state. Part of what makes that possible is confidence, since I've done the thing before. Otherwise, the entire spell would crumble around my ears, no matter how much sauce I have."

Albert whistled. "That's a lot of energy to handle."

"It is. I don't want to make it sound easy. This one spell has taken me years of practice."

"Because of how hard it is or because of the danger of the spell collapsing?"

"Both. First, I had to develop my fluency in Maxwell, which Dr. Watson provided me. It took time and effort, but it happened. Then I had to practice. I had to build my Will and my skill simultaneously. Because nobody wants to screw around with time."

Dani sipped her coffee. "You got that right. Now, Albert, what do you take away from all this?"

The Spaniard sat back in his chair and thought for a long moment. "I think it means I need to be careful."

"Yes. Why?"

"Oh! I know this one," interjected the imp.

Dani pointed a finger at the imp. "H.H., please. Go ahead, Albert."

"Because it isn't just chemistry like you suggested earlier. It's more like nuclear power. Making it is the easy part; I mean, once you know how. Controlling it is what gets people in trouble."

"Exactly."

CHAPTER SEVEN

Columbo, Sri Lanka

Janice leaned on the wall of the balcony. She was cautiously feeding bits of banana to a monkey that, if not tame, was a regular visitor to her sessions with Cassandra. As promised, scrying the distant past had become easier, but even so, the effort left her drained. After each attempt, her sleep was black and dreamless. The glimpses had fascinated her but stirred up more questions than they'd answered. Her new mentor promised to address some of them today.

After seizing the last bit of banana, the monkey screeched and leapt away. Almost on cue, Cassandra stepped onto the balcony and gestured for Janice to join her at the table.

"You have questions. Start with whichever troubles you most."

Janice bit her lip. Everything felt so intertwined that it was hard to know where to begin.

"There's so much I never thought about. Magic is taught at universities alongside the other arts and sciences."

Cassandra smiled. "I had a hand in that, but unless it concerns you, that's a tale for another day."

"You... No, wait. How did all this get...normalized? Set in motion?"

"Very good. Cause and effect. You're living in the effect and wondering about the cause."

"I guess."

"Simply put, since the scattering of the *Demon Codex*, practitioners have organized themselves into different groups."

"Groups?"

"Secret societies concerned with protecting the use of magic in the world."

"Are you a part of such a society?"

"I am. We call it Péra. Let me show you."

Janice flinched, but Cassandra waved her concern aside. "I'll do the work this time. Just watch."

Tun Tavern, Philadelphia, 1775

In these uncertain times, Tun Tavern had gained a reputation for meetings both public and clandestine. The two gentlemen who had claimed a table in the back looked no different from the other patrons. Their clothing identified them as prosperous but not wealthy. Their accents marked them as foreign-born or at least well-educated, but Philadelphia had many such gentlemen among its residents and visitors. Even so, they were unlike any others within the confines of the Pennsylvania Colony, saving perhaps Benjamin Franklin. In point of fact, one of the men, Cyrus Lee, had gone to great pains to ensure that Franklin was otherwise engaged.

None of the others in the tavern paid the two men in the back any attention. The pair each had drinks before them and appeared to speak convivially. They shared a joke and pleasantries about the weather, inconspicuously steering clear of the multiple political conversations that were all too commonplace in that day and place. A barmaid paused at their table to refill their mugs, departing with a coin from Cyrus.

Once she was out of earshot, he turned to his guest, the time for chitchat past. "Thank you for meeting me. There are some things best not committed to letters."

"It is no hardship. I have intended to visit this city for months," assured William Bowie. "It was simply a case of stacking up several errands here so I could attend to them all at once. It is fair to say that, much as I love Maryland, a change of scenery now and then makes me appreciate it all the more. Though you should know from the outset, my plan is to return home tomorrow unless our business tonight requires me to extend my stay."

Cyrus lifted his mug, reduced the contents by half, and set it aside. "Then allow me to be direct. By my assessment, there is a disproportionately large number of practitioners living in these colonies. I find them to be more forward-thinking than our brethren in England or throughout Europe."

"I've had similar thoughts regarding our numbers, though I'm unclear about what you mean by 'forward-thinking.'"

"Let me begin to answer that question by posing you a different one. What is your position on Dee?"

"John Dee?"

Cyrus' hand fell upon his mug, but he did not lift it for another drink. "That's the one."

"I think it's fair to say he accelerated and expanded interest in our arts," explained Bowie. "I'm not saying he's the cause of it all, but look how much the world has changed in less than two hundred years."

"And yet we've not seen scholarship on his level in the years since then. I lay the blame for that at the feet of the so-called Followers of St. Andrew. Dee's compilations gave us procedures and details for contacting denizens of the many realms that exist in parallel to ours and sparked a revolution for practitioners. In his quest to find the language of the angels, he acquired mastery of more otherworldly tongues than anyone before or since. Whether by design or intention, the Followers of St. Andrew ended that scholarship.

"By breaking up his masterwork, his *Demon Codex*, and scattering the pieces to the corners of the world, they did more than just block the summoning of those persons from other realms. Yes, they prevented the instability such forces inevitably bring. I contend it resulted in a secondary outcome as well."

"You have something specific in mind?"

Cyrus smiled, pausing to raise his mug to his lips and take a sip. "I do. It is human nature to rebel against what we are told to do—some more than others—but we all experience resistance to instruction, however well-intentioned, from our earliest childhood."

Bowie lifted his own mug, smiling as he drank. "I well remember my childhood resentment to some of my father's edicts, which he delivered with variations on a theme of *his rules under his roof*." He gestured with his mug at the rest of the tavern. "That attitude continues into adulthood and is given freer expression here in the colonies. I have little doubt that they will prevail against George back in England. Is that why you chose this tavern as our meeting place? Even in Maryland, it is known as a gathering place for groups and fraternities with one or another focused purpose, many of which are not friendly to the crown."

"Indirectly," explained Cyrus. "One of the groups you mentioned is the Society of St. Andrew, founded here earlier this year."

The Virginian was nonplussed. "You cannot mean the Followers of St. Andrew?"

"I do not. The name is a happy coincidence. This new group is a benevolent society for those of Scottish ancestry. That similarity, I believe, grants us an added layer of protection for anyone listening for whispers of St. Andrew."

"You fear practitioners of Aoede are eavesdropping on you?"

"I have no doubt," insisted Cyrus. "The proliferation of practitioners of the arts has likewise led to an increase in mistrust. We are individually and collectively choosing sides, independent of the politics driving the mundane world around us."

"I don't disagree," replied Bowie. "Did you invite me here to determine which I have chosen?"

"Quite the contrary. I wanted the opportunity to make a case for my own choice, which is that we should emulate Dee and not content ourselves with what he has already provided."

"How do you mean?"

"It comes down to this. Most of us work with what we learned from Dee. We use Aoede to expand our knowledge of one language or another. We use that knowledge to create artifacts that hold energies not otherwise seen in this world. We specialize, seeking to master, to some extent, one or perhaps two languages beyond the basics of Aoede that we see only as a tool to achieve those goals. That is Dee's legacy as most understand it."

"You see it differently," suggested Bowie.

"I do. I would have us emulate Dee's efforts."

"I'm not following."

"I believe we waste our efforts scrambling to find what has already been learned and hidden. I have no interest in seeking the scattered pieces of *gli Anderlibri*. I consider it a waste of time that our fellow practitioners among the Followers of St. Andrew devote themselves to. They play an endless game of hiding their precious fragments, moving them from place to place to ensure their 'safety.'"

"What would you have us do instead?"

"Be like Dee."

"Are we not?"

"Not even remotely," assured Cyrus. "It is an illusion to think we are making progress when in fact, we are merely gilding what we already know. That's not progress. That's not what Dee pursued, or do you believe we have found all the languages of the heavens?"

"Honestly, I have never considered the question."

"Consider it now or accept my word on the matter. Other realms exist, and the only reason we have not found them is that we have stopped looking."

Bowie responded by draining his mug. He set it aside and caught the eye of the barmaid but waved her off, not wanting a refill and denying Cyrus one as well. "All right, I take your point. Though surely you're well aware that it requires both a profound command of Aoede and an inordinate amount of time to trace through the whisperings and compile even the simplest of grammars or a partial lexicon of a new language."

"Yet, Dee managed to do it many times."

Bowie shrugged. "Who among us would claim to be like Dee in that regard?

"I'm not seeking practitioners who can uncover ten new languages," explained Cyrus. "But I would be glad to find me ten men who are each willing to shine the light on one."

"Is your purpose the benevolent expansion of knowledge?"

"In the long run, yes, but in these troubled times, our fellow scholars with whom we should have common cause align themselves in groups and secret societies that might at some critical moment be at odds with one another. Against that day, I would welcome the tools and unique knowledge that otherwise unknown languages might offer. That is why I asked you here."

Bowie regarded him with quiet intent for several moments. "You wish to start a secret society of your own and would have me as one of its members."

"As to the organization, I have already done so."

"You tell me all this with no fear that I might reject what you offer, let alone betray you to one of the other sides you see as vying for my membership?"

"I don't consider that the likely outcome. Although our association has been brief, and for the main part, confined to necessarily vague letters, I see in you a burning curiosity easily as powerful as my own. Which is why I came here prepared to offer you a tool which will allow you to employ that curiosity in a common direction."

"I confess you've sparked my interest," acknowledged Bowie. "But let us move from vague promises to specifics. What kind of tool?"

Cyrus raised his right hand, palm inward, and with his left index finger, tapped a gold signet ring he wore on his pinky. The ring was small and unadorned, the signet an elaborate swirl that, upon closer inspection, was the inverse of the letters B and D.

"Beyond Dee?" ventured Bowie.

"Just so." Cyrus removed the ring from his finger and set it on the table between them. He reached into the pocket of his coat and withdrew an identical ring, which he placed on his hand.

"Secret societies and matching jewelry," remarked Bowie, keeping his expression light but unable to eliminate the scorn from his words. "Are there other trappings?"

"You will not be so flippant once you understand that this is more than jewelry. This is the tool I spoke of."

Bowie picked up the ring but did not put it on. He held it in the palm of his hand, studying it, then lifted his gaze to his companion. "You do not know me as well as you might, so I think it is fair to say you did not have advanced knowledge of my impatience for games. Our conversation borders on the tedious now. If you have something to say, I pray you, say it and spare me your attempts at dramatic tension."

If he was put off by Bowie's bluntness, Cyrus gave no sign. "The ring is an artifact that I have personally constructed."

"I surmised as much," replied Bowie. He paused a moment and added, "Of what nature?"

"It facilitates the use of Aoede."

"That's not possible." Bowie frowned. "Even before the scattering of the *Demon Codex*, those who had read the section on Aoede found nothing they could do to enhance its use beyond the simplest directions for how to focus and narrow the range of whispers the practitioner attended to."

"That has changed," explained Cyrus.

"You've enhanced the focus?"

"Indirectly. I've lowered the background noise."

"What do you mean?"

"To use the ring, you must still be quite fluent in Aoede. Then, more than just selecting the parameters of the whispers you wish to attend to, when you find a word or phrase that is your goal, you can cause all voices other than the one who spoke those words to fall away, their whispers no longer competing with what you want to hear."

Bowie's fingers closed into a fist, capturing the ring. "You've created a spying device. With such a tool, an ally of the crown could identify, say, the voice of General Washington. You might hear his plans, learn his resources, or gain advanced knowledge as to the movement of his troops."

"That's true," admitted Cyrus. "But that would not take us beyond Dee."

"How then would you have me use it?"

"Find a word or phrase, a whisper from a realm not previously identified. Apply the ring's focus to that speaker and bring us knowledge of new beings and the powers they open to us."

"You are certain I would use this tool to expand our knowledge of the arts and not apply its use to political gains?"

"The two are not mutually exclusive, which I admit is a risk, but I suspect I can appeal to your curiosity."

"My curiosity?"

"We will always have politics. That too is human nature, but so is curiosity. For the right people, by which I mean the group I am building, that curiosity manifests in the desire to know what has not previously been known in our world."

"To acquire languages beyond those identified by John Dee," stated Bowie. It was not a question.

Cyrus smiled. "Do we possess a more powerful trait than curiosity?"

CHAPTER EIGHT

The Summer Palace, Beijing, China
Watson wandered the paths along the top of Longevity Mountain, avoiding the majority of visitors taking the other routes to the Pavilion of Precious Clouds. Oblivious to most of his surroundings, he focused on repeatedly putting one foot in front of the other in an attempt to stay awake. The chilly weather helped, but even the chattering of his teeth and the discomfort of the wind cutting through his clothes could only do so much. He hadn't slept a wink on the flight, deciding instead to use the time to reach out to more of his former students, and the jet lag had caught up with him.

Maybe a nap would have been smart.

It had been years since he'd pushed himself this hard, and he had fallen back on habits from his younger days. After landing and clearing Customs, Watson had taken a taxi to the Hilton. A shower and fresh clothes had made him feel better and provided enough energy to get into another taxi and travel to the Summer Palace.

That had been a mistake. Sitting in the back of the taxi on the way to his rendezvous had erroneously convinced his body it was time to rest. Now, twenty minutes later, he found himself wandering in the dappled sunlight and the surprisingly bitter cold, half-asleep.

"Derrick?"

Watson turned and smiled when he recognized Dr. Patrice Wu, one of his former graduate assistants who was now a professor in her own right. She specialized in magical antiquities and had achieved high status in her field in a short span of time.

A slight woman, Patrice barely came up to Watson's chest. She had dressed for the cold weather in a Burberry coat and wool slacks. A teal scarf draped her neck, and her cheeks were lightly flushed from the wind. Her straight black hair billowed about her shoulders as she came forward with a smile.

"Patrice, it's great to see you."

"And you, but I'm confused. To what do I owe the honor, and why the secrecy? You do realize that academics having clandestine gatherings is frowned upon here, right?"

Watson rubbed his face. "Yeah. I'm sorry about the urgency, as well as the cloak and dagger stuff. Something bad has happened."

Patrice's eyes narrowed with concern. "Well, whatever it is, let me help. Do you want to sit down? You look exhausted."

Watson chuckled and shook his head. "If I sit down, I'll fall asleep. Let's walk."

Patrice fell into step with him, and they continued down the wooded path near the top of Longevity Mountain.

"Do you remember my old friend Iosefa Malifa?"

"The necromancer with a big head and even bigger belly? The one they call 'Fat Mage?'"

Watson gave a little smile. "That's him."

"Sure. Is he okay?"

He sighed. "No. He's not. In fact, he's now a lich."

Patrice stopped. Watson continued a few steps, paused, and came back. She grabbed his arm. "He's a *what*?"

"A lich."

"I know what a lich is, Derrick, at least theoretically. Where did he get the power to pull it off? How can you be sure?"

"Because I saw him do it. He perfected his design of soul bottles. Then he somehow got his hands on several pages of the *Demon Codex*."

"I know the Codex is real, but it's been lost for so long. I've always thought of it as a cautionary tale, more myth than reality for contemporary practitioners."

"I wish it were, but it's very real. Malifa now possesses more of it than anyone since the Renaissance."

Patrice shook her head. "Okay, I get that this is terrible and frightening, but what does it have to do with me? I specialize in magical artifacts of the past, but the pieces of the *Demon Codex* were never something I've come across. Is that what you've come all this way to talk to me about?"

"No, it's more basic than that. Malifa isn't done. I am convinced that he is hunting for the rest of the *Codex,* and he's using my past students to help him do it. His use of soul bottles ensures that they will aid him, willingly or not."

They resumed walking. She brought a hand up to cup her chin, tapping her cheek with her index finger. "Hmm. This might explain the uptick in new versions of soul bottles that have appeared on both the black market and the dark web over the last year. They weren't antiquities so I lost interest, though the number available was noteworthy. Anyway, it didn't last. It was just an anomaly that went away about a month ago."

Watson looked up to notice they'd passed the Buddhist Tower of Incense and arrived at the Summer Palace's majestic Pavilion of Precious Clouds. The magnificent structure was also known as the Bronze Pavilion and was once home to a statue of Buddha that emperors and empresses prayed to. He cast his imagination back across the centuries and let his tired eyes enjoy the grandeur of the architecture, but only for a moment.

"Malifa told us he'd perfected his soul bottles by releasing different prototypes onto the black market and letting other practitioners risk themselves to uncover whatever flaws those early versions contained. Then he'd correct them and iterate the process."

"You're saying he crowdsourced his research and development?"

Watson grunted his assent. "That was probably the bump you saw. Once he perfected his methodology, he'd have cleared away the failed versions and moved on."

"Who else is involved? Or was this just between the two of you?"

"No. As I mentioned, he dragged some of my former students into it. Lured them to him with pieces of the *Codex* and took control of them."

"Who are they? Who else knows about this?"

Watson shook his head. "I'd rather not say."

Patrice started to reply or argue the point, but she stopped and simply shrugged. "Okay. I'm sure you have your reasons, but if you won't talk to me, you made a very long trip for very little gain."

They'd stopped again. The wind had picked up, and the cold cut through him worse than before. Watson stretched his back and groaned. He took a deep breath and let his gaze wander toward Kunming Lake and the Palace's Stone Boat, allowing himself to be distracted, if only for a moment, by the many sights and their history. "Some stories aren't mine to share. What I *can* say is that Malifa was using soul bottles as part of a scheme involving pieces of *gli Anderlibri* that he'd recovered, and he is actively trying to track down more of them."

"It's that last part that brought you to see me."

"After your doctoral defense, you thought you had a lead on a hiding place for a piece of the *Demon Codex*. I was worried that Malifa might target you next."

"You could have just called and saved yourself a lengthy trip."

"Some things are better done face-to-face, especially if he'd already gotten to you. I needed to see for myself."

Patrice crossed her arms, her expression severe. "What would you have done if he had?"

Watson demurred. "I'm glad he didn't, but I would have done everything in my power to help you."

"Well, I can assure you that Fat Mage hasn't contacted me, and I can't imagine that he would try. Certainly not here. The government is not keen on magic users, and they keep an eye on them. Besides, I haven't practiced in years. I've been too focused on my research into the historical and archaeological record to devote time to spellcraft."

"Then I'm sorry I bothered you, Patrice. It was good to see your face and confirm that you're safe."

Patrice watched Watson wander downhill, unfolding a map of the Palace grounds as he went. She waited until he'd passed out of view before she went down a side path and checked for signs of surveillance. Only then did she pull out her phone. She activated an encrypted voice application and put the phone to her ear.

After two beeps, a metallic voice came over the line.

"Specify a recipient and leave a message."

Beep.

"This is the Custodian. My message is for the Librarian. You were right. Derrick Watson is indeed in China. He came to visit me with a story about a necromancer whom he claims has found some of *gli Anderlibri* and is actively seeking more of them.

"It could be true, or he could be delusional. Worst case, it's an elaborate distraction, and he is the Scorpion we've known would eventually appear, though I'm not inclined to believe that—not yet. It seems too convenient, and in this matter, we need to be certain.

"He might simply be a good man and not the monster we've been expecting. I'd rather you didn't kill him unless we're all convinced and in agreement. Put out the word to the others. It is time to assemble the council. I'll join the rest of the Folio in Tuscany in three days."

CHAPTER NINE

<u>Alexander University, Philadelphia</u>

The setting sun painted the Humanities building in warm light as Albert flung open the door and bounded up the steps to the second floor. His familiar clung to his shirt collar for dear life as the young mage all but skipped into the outer office of the Department of Demonic Languages. He held a pizza box in one hand, and in the other, he gripped a bottle of merlot discreetly hidden within a brown paper bag. He crossed the foyer and let himself into Professor Watson's office without knocking, as he had for several months since the weekly ritual with his mentor had begun.

Instead of his mentor, he found Trixie. The professor's girlfriend sat on the office's couch with books and notepads spread in front of her and the unmistakable tracks of recent tears on her cheeks.

"Oh! Trixie, I'm sorry. I didn't mean to interrupt."

The undergrad wiped at her face and smiled. It looked like a forced smile, but Albert wasn't about to say so.

"No. It's okay, Albert. Derrick's not here. I'm sorry. I was supposed to tell Petrini to let you know he was away. I guess I forgot. Also, well, I just needed a place to study."

"Oh." Albert sighed, crestfallen and annoyed. Something else was happening, and he kept the disappointment out of his voice when he asked, "Where is he?"

"Beijing...and Iceland too, I think. He blew through his sabbatical funds to cover the airline tickets, then ran off to search for more pieces of the *Demon Codex*."

"Is that why you're upset? I thought we all agreed he needed to go."

"I'm not upset about that. I thought he was doing these things alone, but I'm giving him the benefit of the doubt because the costs were so high. No, I'm upset because he's a stupid man. I offered to go with and empty my savings, but it wouldn't have helped. He had a visa from the Chinese government and I don't. They wouldn't have let me in."

From Albert's shoulder, H.H. nodded in agreement and shared his unsolicited opinion. "I could have told you stupidity is a common trait among humans."

"Shhh," Albert hissed. He asked Trixie, "Is that all of it, or is there something else? A problem with passports isn't worth crying over. What else did he do?"

"What did he do? He did the worst thing ever. He proposed!"

"Wow."

"Yeah! Wow."

"You're upset because you don't love him?"

"What? No! I'm upset because I *do* love him. I hurt his feelings, and now I can't get in touch with him to try to make things better. I'm upset because I'm in love with him, or I think I am, but his timing was terrible. I'm not where I need to be in life. This is all happening too fast and too soon. I mean, *way* ahead of schedule. Though, what does that schedule mean? Does life respect our plans? Does any of it matter? Is it fair to either of us to expect love to work according to my calendar?"

Albert's ears were going numb, but he figured it was best to let Trixie ramble. Clearly, she was still working things out.

H.H. shook its tiny head from its perch on Albert's shoulder. "The more time I spend on this plane, the more convinced I am that humans are hardwired to make themselves and each other miserable."

"H.H., shut up and go wait in my office."

"Fine. I didn't want pizza anyway. It gives me gas."

The imp scampered down Albert's back and dashed out of Watson's office, flattening itself to slip under the door.

Albert placed the pizza and wine on the professor's desk and pulled Watson's chair out from behind it.

As Trixie continued to vent, he fetched paper plates and plastic cups from a file drawer. Much as he would have done if Watson had been there for their weekly review, he dished out the pie and poured a couple of glasses of wine.

He offered one of each to Trixie. The alchemy student broke off her monologue, sniffled once, and accepted. She wolfed down the slice in seconds and sheepishly gestured for a second. Albert quickly complied.

"Thanks. I didn't realize how hungry I was."

Albert nodded as he pulled the chair closer and took a seat across from her. "No problem. Somebody has to eat it, and Professor Watson isn't here to help. His loss."

Trixie smirked. "Hey, what did you come to talk to him about? Pizza and wine? Are you celebrating? You had a big grin on your face when you came through the door."

"We do this once a week. The professor calls it a seminar, though technically, I've finished my course work and am supposed to be writing my dissertation. We meet and kick around ideas, trying to come up with something that's a good fit for me. It's always interesting, but nothing's come of it yet. Today would have been different."

"Different how?"

"It's a long story."

"I've got time." She sighed. "Besides, I've been doing all the talking. It's my turn to listen for a while."

Albert shrugged. "I've had a breakthrough with my magic. I stopped taking my ADHD medications after the incident with Malifa like Dani recommended, and my Will started to come back in a big way."

"That's wonderful, Albert. I'm happy for you."

"Thanks, but it's also kinda scary. I've never tried to handle this much power."

Trixie nodded. "I get that. You do know you're Derrick's best student, right? Maybe ever. He's told me so."

Albert looked shocked. "Really?"

"Yep. He loves you."

Albert's face reddened. Rather than respond, he plunged back into his explanation. "Anyway, I went out to the puppy farm and spent a couple of days with Dani and Stanley. They helped me with some magical theory I'd been missing."

"You hadn't learned magical theory?"

"I had, but I've never fully understood it. It didn't make sense while my Will was retarded. It never…clicked."

"Ah, gotcha. Go on."

"So, I worked with Stanley, studying the creation of magical building blocks like the ones he uses in Maxwell. That isn't something I would use since that's not a language I'm interested in, but I saw how the concept worked, and I've been applying it to a language I know well—Centzontōtōchtin."

"That's the language of illusion, right? Named for the drunk rabbits?"

"Yep."

"Okay, but explain what you mean by building blocks."

"Well, Centzontōtōchtin, like several demonic tongues, is an agglutinative language. That means complex words can be created by stringing together lots of distinct, meaningful bits."

"I studied German on an app. You're talking about how they mash smaller words together to form really long single words."

"Close enough."

"Okay, go on."

"As a result, I've created some really cool illusions. After I work out the specifics, I can pretty much just hang them in place, ready to go. That means I can cast them in record time with almost no effort by using the same root and only making minor substitutions, sometimes only a syllable or two, and using bursts of Will to force the change through."

"Cool. Can I see?"

"Sure."

Albert began speaking, and a moment later, his face was replaced by the visage of Stanley Chen.

"That's great!"

"Not yet. That's the basic part. I really wanted the professor to see me rework it on the fly. That's the thing that's impressive. Watch."

Stanley spoke two words, and his appearance changed to that of Dani Lefevere. Two words later, his face mirrored Trixie's down to the puffy eyes and tear tracks.

"Ack! I look terrible. Make it go away."

Albert laughed and dropped the illusion.

"Albert, that's amazing. Not just for you, but for any mage. You've really made a breakthrough."

He shrugged off the praise. "It's just about focus and preparation. Once I've memorized and practiced the core of the spell to the point that it's automatic, it is about my Will and my ability to sustain the spell."

"Well, Derrick will be duly impressed. I have no doubt."

"Thanks. By the way, did he say when he'd be back?"

Trixie shrugged. "Probably. I was frazzled by his proposal. He's making a loop. First China, then Iceland, then back home. He did say something about a yeti."

"A what?"

"Yeah, that was my reaction as well."

CHAPTER TEN

Liberty Plaza, Philadelphia

Her flight from Sri Lanka was in the air for twenty hours, plus a six-hour layover in Qatar. Cassandra had used that delay to pay a surprise visit to a Péra operative in Doha and noted that the man was living too well in an ultra-modern apartment with more bedrooms than he needed. If she was overly harsh, she reflected it was a consequence of the lengthy first half of her flight. To compensate and restore her mood, she stopped in and whiled away a couple of hours at the Museum of Islamic Art before returning to the airport and, eventually, Philadelphia.

Between training her new protégé and staying abreast of developments among the other secret societies, she couldn't recall a time when she'd used so much Everett in so short a span. She assumed they were tracking Péra but were limited to using Aoede to listen in rather than scrying. She stayed informed of the location of every Everett speaker, even those loyal to other organizations, and she had wards in place against all of them. It was daunting but manageable. There weren't many.

On a whim, she'd gone from the airport to downtown Philadelphia and visited that symbol of American independence, the Liberty Bell. It was still cracked, but she had expected it to be.

It had rained earlier, scattering the tourists, but the sun had since come out. She sat on a bench on the plaza. Staring at a puddle, Cassandra indulged herself and studied the past. As she had observed, it had a tendency to repeat itself.

Paris, France, 1783

The door of a private room at the Hôtel d'York opened, and David Hartley, one of the king's representatives at the negotiations, slipped in to join the other four men.

"You're alone." Romney scowled. "Where is Franklin?"

"He's not coming," replied Hartley, "and I can't stay long. We'll be signing the treaty tomorrow, and there are far too many eyes for us both to slip away at the same time, let alone together."

Another of the four, John Petty, spoke up. His Irish accent was slight but caused his words to stand out in any conversation. "With respect, sir, it was Franklin's idea that the six of us gather. We have done so over our shared concerns about Dee's book. I thought we had an agreement that this matter far outweighed even American independence—"

Hartley cut him off. "Then I suggest we get straight to it. I have a letter from Franklin, stating that I speak with his voice as well as my own in these matters. Let us accomplish what we may in the time we have."

Charles Romney looked around the room. "Very well." He paused and gathered his thoughts. "We five are long since known to one another through correspondence and occasional meetings. Two of you have been guests of the Folio. However, I believe this is the first time we've gathered in one room. It is fair to say we are the most proficient speakers of Aoede the world has ever known."

"Certainly the most proficient since Dee and his damn book," remarked Thomas Clarkson, who was in his early twenties and the youngest of the men present.

"But unlike Dee," continued Romney, "instead of using our abilities to explore the language of angels, we have eavesdropped on the secrets of men to our own benefit and the political advantages of our nations."

"It is time to take a more global view. It comes back to Dee," replied Hartley.

"I don't disagree," acknowledged Clarkson, "which is why I and a group of like-minded scholars I represent seek to reassemble the scattered sections of that book."

A chill passed through the room as all present recognized that Romney and Clarkson represented opposite extremes, and not simply as a consequence of Romney being twice the younger mage's age.

"Whereas I and my own colleagues and students are dedicated to ensuring those pieces remain both scattered and hidden," insisted Romney.

"What good does that do anyone?" asked Clarkson.

"It protects humanity. The restoration of Dee's *Codex* is part of a prophecy we gleaned through the use of Aoede."

"Prophecy?" Clarkson scoffed. "This is the first time I am hearing about a prophecy. You're the Folio's so-called Librarian. Tell me what this prophecy has to do with the book."

"The prophecy speaks of the arrival of a practitioner we call the Scorpion, an individual of learning and power. When he appears, he will be unable to deny his true nature and will threaten the entire world. We have reason to believe his strategies will include the summoning of a being or beings from one or more other realms. As such, we stand in opposition to anyone with the intention of re-gathering the fragments of Dee's book."

"That simply?" asked Thomas. "What, you'd call a war down on your opposition? Scholar versus scholar? Should we now fear that our fellow speakers of Aoede will use their skill to listen in on one another?"

"You'd be a fool not to be doing so already," responded Hartley. "Given the conversations some here have already spied on for various mundane political factions."

"That is unsupportable," sputtered the Irishman.

"Yet true," replied Hartley with a long look at Petty. "Though I have mentioned no names. Franklin and I have long suspected such. To test the matter, over the years, we have knowingly discussed critical information from our research that was fraudulent but would lead to specific conclusions and actions. By observing those actions, we have been able to see who among you was listening in."

Petty glared at him, tight-lipped.

"Please," pleaded Romney. "We are trying to ensure the survival of scholars like ourselves and establish common goals that transcend national borders and political goals."

"That's very high-minded," responded Clarkson, "but it also conveniently would have us end our respective pursuit of the pages of Dee's book and the power they would bring."

"I am authorized to offer compensation," replied Romney.

Hartley's head swung toward the Librarian in surprise. "Compensation? There's been no mention of such a thing before."

"My apologies." Romney briefly bowed his head and then added, "We only achieved consensus on the matter last night."

"We?"

"The leaders of the Folio."

"What kind of compensation?" asked Clarkson.

"In our efforts to keep the pieces of Dee's book hidden, we've come into possession of a folio he wrote that provides detailed instructions for creating permanent books."

"That's impossible," responded Petty in disbelief. "That folio hasn't been seen since the initial scattering at Montale. My fellow

Followers of St. Andrew have searched for it for more than one hundred and fifty years without success."

"We found it in Tunis," explained Romney, "in the burned-out remains of what I was told was a brothel. I will spare you the sordid details of how we believe it arrived there and remained hidden for so long. In exchange for your sworn oath not to impede the mission of my companions, I am empowered to offer each of you your own copy."

Quiet filled the small room. The four other men gazed at Romney. He could almost hear the gears within their minds turning. Hartley broke the silence. "I speak for both Franklin and myself when I say I would willingly take such an oath if it meant we would once again have the means to preserve our writings for all time."

Clarkson snorted. "Or at least until such time as the whore you are bedding has her brothel catch fire."

Petty ignored him. "Why should we believe these alleged copies can create permanent volumes?"

Romney responded with a broad smile, "Each copy has undergone the procedures described within it. Each is, in itself, a permanent book."

"A strong incentive indeed," murmured Pietro Agricola, the fifth man in the room. He had been silent up to this point. Despite his heavy Italian accent, he spoke with a scholar's calm assurance and the egotistical certainty of a popular painter with highly placed patrons in the Catholic church. "But I will not take your folio if it means turning aside from my desire to bring together the scattered pieces of Dee's work. The man was a genius, a visionary far ahead of his time. It was the fear of lesser minds that led to the partitioning and hiding of his great work."

"I respect your position and can only pray that you respect mine." Romney sighed.

Clarkson glanced at Agricola as if sensing an ally, then replied to Romney, "Let me be clear. I will not go out of my way to obstruct your efforts, nor will I tolerate obstruction of my own. I and the like-minded scholars I work with will continue to seek the fragments of Dee's work with the express intention of reassembling them."

"Then you are a fool," stated Petty. He turned away from the younger man and responded to Romney's proposal. "For my part and the people I represent, I accept your terms. There is too much destruction in the world, and if Dee's alchemy can be used to preserve what we currently have against future loss, it is a price worth paying."

Clarkson glowered at the Irishman, then turned to look at Agricola as if for support. The object of his gaze did not return it, choosing to stare at his hands and absently tug at a pinkie ring. The moment passed, and Clarkson, like a petulant child, went back to glaring at Romney.

"I agree," said Hartley. "And I've no doubt that Franklin, master of innovation that he is, would likewise agree. The process as outlined in your folio would be a great boon for his new nation."

"Assuming you manage to get that treaty signed tomorrow," offered Agricola softly.

"Have no fear on that score," replied Hartley. "Besides, we agreed to hold ourselves above conversations about politics in this gathering."

The Italian shrugged his acceptance. "You're the one who brought it up, sir."

"We are short on time. I would call this vote. I hear one who is opposed," acknowledged Romney, "and three in agreement, albeit one by proxy. What do you say, Agricola?"

"I say it is a strong inducement that you offer, and I hope that although I feel the need to pass at this time, you will again extend the offer to me and mine at a future date."

"Why would you delay?"

"I have not used Aoede to spy on my fellow practitioners." He paused, and with an encompassing gesture, included the other four in the room. "Rather, I have listened to sounds, words, and phrases never spoken in our world. Much I imagined as John Dee must have done for years to assemble his book."

"What have you heard?" asked Hartley.

"A unique language." He smiled as he spoke. "One not heard by anyone in this room, though I am informed by Catholic priests in the New World that the natives there have had knowledge of it for a hundred years."

"That's preposterous," insisted Clarkson. "Dee's list of the languages of other realms is exhaustive."

"Apparently not," murmured the Italian.

"What if you are in error?" asked Hartley

Agricola shrugged. "I will waste my time with no impact on you and yours."

"I fail to see how refraining from the pursuit of Dee's original texts will impede your efforts in this supposed new language." Romney's hope for gaining Agricola's support was palpable.

"Let us say I would rather not reinvent what has already been created," replied Agricola. "I seek a piece of Dee's original *Codex*, not to utilize the power it might convey, but rather as a template on which to draft a document outlining this new language."

Romney appeared to chew on the Italian's words. "That is an unexpected argument." He considered the situation and, after a few moments, locked eyes with the Italian. "You are not in direct opposition to our goals."

"I am not," agreed Agricola. "I hope you are not in a position to oppose mine."

"Perhaps we can come to an accommodation," suggested Charles, adopting a softer tone. "A fair copy of one of the fragments that does not contain within it the mechanisms to utilize its knowledge that is bound into the pages of the original."

"That would be a fine start," replied Agricola. "Though for all I know, those mechanics might be a necessary piece of the template I seek. We can discuss these things as they occur."

"I'm open to that." Romney continued, "I will count your response as an abstention and content myself with the three who agree to my proposition."

"I do not mean for us to go to war," insisted Clarkson, though whether he was sincere or merely contrite was unclear.

"That would be a terrible waste on all sides," agreed Agricola.

"I must be getting back." Hartley rose from his seat. "My absence is likely to have been noted by now."

Romney shrugged. "I have no other business. I thank you all for gathering. I feel we have accomplished a good amount this evening, both in our agreements and in shedding light on our differences."

"Wait a moment, please," requested Clarkson and turned to address Agricola. "What is this new language?"

"It was discovered by a priest of the Aztec people," explained Pietro Agricola. "He called it 'Centzontōtōchtin,' which is a reference to one hundred drunken rabbit deities in their mythology."

Several struggled to shape the name with their mouths.

"Drunken rabbits?" asked Hartley, trying and failing to keep the amusement out of his voice.

"A hundred, yes," stated the Italian scholar as if the number were obvious.

"A brace of conies wouldn't have been enough?"

Agricola shrugged.

"What is the domain of this new language?" asked Petty.

The Italian smiled. "Centzontōtōchtin is a language of illusion," he murmured and followed this statement with a long string of syllables never before heard on the European continent. Then he disappeared from view as if he'd never been in the room.

CHAPTER ELEVEN

Durgo's Realm of Yum

Trixie sat in her favorite booth at Durgo's, picking at a basket of French fries and absently using the tips of the golden tubers to smear ketchup in random patterns across the basket's paper lining. She gazed out the window, watching the leaves swirl by outside, and she waited. It didn't take long. Dani pulled her car into the parking lot and walked through the door a moment later.

Trixie stood up, waved to attract Dani's attention, and hugged her the instant she came within range. The older woman dropped her coat into the booth, and they sat down.

"Did you want to order something?"

"No, I'm good, thanks." Dani shook her head even as she eyed Trixie's fries.

Trixie grinned and pushed the basket to the middle of the table. "Best thing on the menu. I've got plenty, and I'm happy to share."

Dani laughed and reached into the basket. "Well, if you insist. Wow, this place brings back a lot of memories."

"Did you come here when you were a student?"

"It opened the year I started on my dissertation. Believe it or not, it was quieter than the office I shared with two other grad students. I wrote some of my best work here."

"You did your doctoral work on Morphello?"

"I did."

"How did you get interested in transmogrification?"

Dani shrugged. "Both my parents are physicians, but neither has more than a droplet of Will and when they had me tested and discovered I registered in the top five percent, they pushed me away from the traditional medical school track. That was fine since I still wanted to heal people's bodies and save lives, but to be honest, it started out selfishly since I was the primary patient I had in mind."

"Wow."

"Yeah. Was that why you wanted to talk?"

Trixie nodded as she drowned another fry in ketchup and popped it into her mouth. "Kinda. I want to understand the relationship between your specialty with Morphello and the physical change it brings about and my area of study, alchemy, and the way it produces change."

Dani's eyebrows rose. "That's a good question. I've never really thought about it. The disciplines have always been isolated. I didn't take any alchemy after my freshman intro course, so I can't speak to any of the subtleties of the field, just basic theory. I suppose the biggest difference is that when you transform something with Morphello, that change is almost always permanent, whereas alchemical changes are typically short-lived."

Trixie reached for another fry but paused, weighing what she'd just heard. "Well, that, and I guess there are a lot more people who understand how to do basic alchemy than speak Morphello."

Dani smiled. "Don't be so certain. I'm pretty sure the basic structures you use in alchemy are rooted in Morphello, just a watered-down, safer-to-use version."

Trixie pulled her backpack off the bench beside her and rifled through it to find a red journal. She opened it to a page overflowing with alchemical formulas and meticulous step-by-step notes, then turned it around so Dani could see.

Dani studied it, tracing the lines of the equations with the tip of her finger. She gave a low whistle. "Wow, Trixie. This is complex stuff."

"It's all alchemy. It's an idea I've been working on."

Dani tapped a section of Trixie's notes near the bottom of the page. "Yeah, that's what I thought."

"What?"

"Well, here's the thing they don't teach you in alchemy that you need to know. In the Morphello realm, nothing is fixed. Everything there, by which I mean matter and time and space, is constantly in flux. You can see that as either obvious or deeply ironic, but as a result, using the language isn't about describing a thing. It's about insisting on it."

"I don't understand."

"It's fundamental. If you accept that everything is in flux, then by extension, transformation isn't about making something from nothing. It's about locking down a single instance from a universe of possibilities. It requires you to impose your idea of reality on the raw stuff of it. The change occurs because, at some level, you believe it's always been that way. When you speak Morphello to produce a change in a thing, you impose your notion on it. It's a very assertive language that relies on more Will than most others."

She spun the journal back around and drew Trixie's attention to the line she'd identified. "But see here, the piece you brought? It's subjunctive."

"Subjunctive?"

"An annoying tense that a lot of languages have and most people don't care about understanding. It's used to describe things not as they are, but as you wish or imagine they might be."

"That doesn't sound very assertive."

Dani grinned. "It's not. It's also why beginning alchemy students who screw up the pronunciation don't get hit with the kind of magical backlash you'd experience with other languages. The subjunctive takes some of the bite out of it. I suspect it's also a large part of why alchemical transformation is temporary."

Trixie chewed her lip in thought for several beats before bobbing her head in understanding. "That makes sense."

"Did you drag me down here to ply me with fries just so you could show me your workbook?"

"Not entirely."

"I didn't think so. I'm guessing that was kind of a combination preamble and icebreaker."

"Pretty much."

"Okay, so stipulated. The ice is broken, and we're running low on fries, so spill it."

Trixie took a deep breath and let it out in a rush along with her words. "Derrick proposed. I simultaneously want to kiss him and kill him."

"Ah. Well, I'm not sure I can be much help. I don't understand Derrick on that level, though I was smitten with him myself when I was a student."

"Did you…"

"Whoa! No. Derrick's never been with a student. Well, not before you, and certainly not one of his own. He just wasn't interested. While he'd be blind to miss how pretty you are, I suspect the stuff in your notebook is at least as attractive to him as your butt in those yoga pants is."

"Most guys aren't like that."

"Most guys aren't Derrick Watson. When I was a student, many of the older professors acted like sex with undergrads was written into their contracts. I think that's changed. Even the old guard among the faculty is mostly woke nowadays, but dallying with co-eds has a long history."

"So, am I an idiot for wanting to wait? Not for someone else, just for more time."

"No. Of course not. You're young. Listen to your heart. If it's too soon, it's too soon. Just remember to communicate. Don't screw this up because you get stuck in your own head."

Trixie nodded. "Too late."

"Not with Derrick. You're lucky. If you talk to him, he'll listen, and he'll really hear you. Besides, I think you guys make a great couple."

Trixie sighed. "Yeah? Try telling that to my parents."

Trixie lingered a few minutes after Dani left, pausing to get back in line and order a burger to bring back to her dorm. Takeout bag in hand, she had just approached the door of her truck and pulled out her keys when she sensed someone walking up to her. She shifted the key in her hand so it stuck out between her knuckles like a spike, then turned around and saw a man in a dark coat coming toward her.

She dropped into a fighting stance and prepared to scream, as she'd been taught.

The man stopped and held up his hands. One of them contained a badge. "Whoa! Whoa, Miss Gallagher. We've met. I'm Agent Colton. I just want to talk to you."

Trixie dropped her hands but kept her glare. "You thought sneaking up on a female college student in a parking lot was the way to go about it? Do they teach that brilliant technique at mage cop surveillance school?"

Colton chuckled and nodded. "You are absolutely right. I'm sorry. I should have thought it through. I just wanted to have a word in private with you."

"About what?"

"About Derrick Watson. What else?"

"You want me to snitch on my boyfriend?"

Colton cocked his head to the side. "Is there something to snitch about?"

Trixie looked nonplused. "No."

"I just want to find out where he is. He hasn't been seen around the university for a while. I know he's on sabbatical, so that makes sense, but he's not answering his phone either."

"You tried calling him?"

Colton shrugged.

"Agent Colton, last I heard, you mage cops don't have an unlimited budget. There are a lot of bad guys out there. Maybe you should spend your time looking for them and leave Derrick alone."

Without another word, Trixie unlocked and then climbed into her truck. She slammed the door, and a moment later, she gunned the engine,

Colton stepped out of the way and watched as she drove off.

CHAPTER TWELVE

Beijing, China

Watson tossed and turned in his hotel bed. Between the jet lag and the über-soft pillows he'd fluffed multiple times, he should have fallen fast asleep. However, not only did sleep refuse to arrive, but its absence actively tormented and aggravated the hell out of him.

After the usual attempts at progressive muscle relaxation, counting sheep, and mentally tagging all the buildings on campus forward and backward, he gave up and turned on the light. He'd brought two books in his carry-on bag, obscure paperbacks from micro presses that didn't traffic in digital copies and so didn't lend their wares to electronic readers or phone apps.

Watson had read the first before they'd served dinner on the flight over but hadn't quite finished the second before landing. He'd tried to read for a bit when he'd first gotten into bed but had set the book aside after less than a page. Fatigue had made his attention wander, and he'd convinced himself that sleep was the better choice.

It would have been had it not proved elusive. Hoping his first instinct had been right, he opened the book but again found he couldn't concentrate. It was worse than before; the words on the page slipped out of his awareness, leaving no memory of what he'd just read. He dropped the book on the bedside table and swore softly.

Was it possible he was so tired that he was beyond sleep? Defeated, Watson rubbed his eyes with his fists, which was why he heard rather than saw the extra-dimensional portal open across the room.

Surprised and very much awake, Watson pushed the covers aside and swung his legs out of bed. Violet light pulsed from a gaping wound on the far wall, pushing back the room's darkness. The glow left the wall and moved closer. Black and purple gas poured out of it when it stopped in front of the hotel room's mini bar. An instant later, the skeletal remains of Iosefa Malifa stepped through. A bony finger tapped a switch on the wall, turning on the hotel room's floor and desk lamps. The glow that had heralded his arrival faded, and the portal closed.

"Don't get up on my account, Derrick. I can see that you're exhausted."

Watson stood anyway, as annoyed at having to confront the lich at all as doing so dressed in only a pair of boxers. "What are you doing here?"

The lich's skull cocked to the side. The green glow from its eye sockets blazed in Watson's direction.

"My old friend, it's simple, really. I came here to chide you for your utter adherence to predictability. I had hoped for more of a challenge from you, but as always, your lack of strategy is exceeded only by the absence of subtlety."

"You plane-walked just to taunt me? That's petty even for you, Iosefa."

"Continue to call me by that name if it brings you comfort, Derrick, but you should know that little of Iosefa Malifa survived my…transition. No, I am not here just to snipe. Quite the opposite. I choose to visit because of my memories of who I was and the affection I felt for you when I wore flesh. Among the many mages in the world, regardless of whether they ply their skills or teach others, practice in solitude, or congregate in mystical societies, until our recent altercation, you were that odd anomaly—a man with great power who chose not to use it."

Watson took a step toward the remains of his friend.

"Did it ever occur to you that *not* using power is the best thing one can do with it?"

Booming laughter filled the room, and the lich ran a bony finger below the eye sockets in its skull as if wiping away a tear.

"Well, no. That thought never occurred to me, not for a second. Nor to anyone else I've known who's ever experienced real power. Only you."

"Why are you here?" Watson repeated. "Surely it's for more than to show me you've worked out how to cause an animated skeleton to laugh."

If the lich noticed the jibe, it showed no sign. "I am continuing my plans to amass more power. More than ever, I can see how wasted it is in the hands of mortal mages, regardless of the realms they draw it from. They are all too weak. Since transcending mere flesh, it galls me how little they do with it."

Watson shrugged. "It's a shame you specialized in Balāṭu. It's clearly colored your view of the living. You're cut off from the truly amazing things mortals can do."

"Don't condescend to *me*, Derrick. I don't need to speak the other languages to access their capabilities. It's far more efficient for me to instead acquire mages with such proficiencies as I find useful. You've seen this firsthand. Control the mages, and I control their power."

"Is that your plan? Steal the souls of every skilled practitioner and bottle them until you need them? Commit an arcane blend of serial abductions and a hostile takeover? You know that won't work. Their bodies can't survive for long. Without a soul, they wither, becoming nothing more than husks. You'll just end up killing them. You of all people know there are easier ways of creating zombies."

The shoulder bones rose and fell in a semblance of a shrug. "I'm not squeamish about the dead, Derrick. As you point out, I've spent a lifetime as a necromancer."

"You're also a pragmatist. Not even a team of necromancers could put souls back into dead bodies. That's all you'd end up with if you collected other practitioners for your future plans."

"You say that like it would be a bad thing. Killing the majority of this world's mages will free up a lot of magical energy. In time, I can seize that for my own use. It's only a beginning, I admit, but one needs to start somewhere."

"This is getting tiresome, Iosefa. Stop trying to impress me. You don't really care what I think. So, I'll ask you one last time, why are you here?"

"Because I need your help. I need access to the beings in other realms to achieve my goals."

"You're still after the pieces of the *Demon Codex*."

"I am, and you will help me obtain them."

Watson scoffed. "Nope. That's not going to happen. You're wasting your time."

Malifa laughed. "I didn't say you'd *choose* to aid me, but as I arrange the pieces on the board of our latest game, you won't be able to help yourself. I know you, Derrick, perhaps better than you know yourself. You're incapable of doing nothing. You won't sit idly by, and anything you do will ultimately serve my purpose."

"Maybe I'll just stay here in China. I'm officially on sabbatical, and nobody expects me to be anywhere."

"You won't."

"No?"

"No. Not now that I've told you my intentions with respect to the rest of *gli Anderlibri*. Being who you are, you will nobly attempt to stand in opposition to me. You'll fail, of course, but your nature won't allow you not to try. Don't rush on my account. As you say, no one expects you to be anywhere. By all means, take in the sights. Get a massage. Taste the local cuisine.

"As I recall, there are some truly extraordinary museums in this city and no shortage of historical sites. Maybe you'll take a trip out to the Great Wall. I know you've always wanted to stand upon it. Go ahead. Take your time. I'm not in too great a hurry, though you should keep in mind that if you choose to delay and force me to wait, I'll distract myself by killing more mages in my pursuit of creating an even better soul bottle. You'll probably blame yourself for their deaths."

"Do you think I'm so easily manipulated?"

"Aren't you? I suppose we'll have to wait and see to know for sure. Good night, Derrick. Get some rest if you can. You have never done air travel well, and I see more of it in your near future."

"You're an oracle now?"

The skeleton clacked its jaw once, then again. "One doesn't need to be conversant in Everett to venture such a prediction."

The lich sketched a mocking bow, and without so much as a gesture or phrase of power, summoned a new portal. It stepped through, vanishing from Watson's hotel room without bothering to turn off the lights. The portal closed with a whoosh.

Watson growled and stomped across the room to slap the switch and restore darkness. He desperately wanted to go back to bed but headed to the bathroom to take a shower instead. It didn't matter how tired he was, there'd be no going back to sleep anytime soon.

CHAPTER THIRTEEN

The Haven, Tuscany
Four people, two women and two men, all skilled practitioners who were well-regarded in their specialties, gathered around an ancient table. The impressive table occupied the center of a private library that was part of an even more impressive estate. A trio of thick-paned windows occupied one wall, providing a low background rumble as rain pounded the glass. The other walls bore endless shelves. Books rose to the peak of the twenty-foot ceiling, where they met massive wood beams that had begun life in the old-growth forests of Prussia three centuries before.

Sparkling water, wine, cheese, dates, and an assortment of chocolates tantalized the senses from the center of the table. The refreshments reflected the highest quality and expense, but the mood did not support socializing or celebration. The atmosphere was somber and heavy as if the impending discussion had cast a shadow upon both the room and its occupants.

A gray-haired scarecrow of a woman motioned for attention. She was only in her fifties, but her clothing—a fine wool suit in an austere and depressing gray with a dashing pink scarf that added a snippet of hope—made her look ten years older. Everything about the woman, every sight and texture, every choice and deliberate gesture, radiated the intersection of refinement and precision.

"Thank you all for coming. To put us on the same page, let me begin by confirming what you suspect. Each of you has independently become aware of an anomaly in the ebb and flow of the world's magical energies."

"It is not this anomaly that concerns me, Madam Librarian," replied an older man, the sense of his words fighting his heavy Russian accent syllable by syllable. "It is the appearance of it as a single source drawing primarily from Centzontōtōchtin, a language that was not among those left to us by Dee and which we rarely see invoked for powerful uses. I have listened to the whispers via Aoede, as have all of you, and I tell you there has never been anything like this in the Catalog.

"I share the Cataloger's concern," added a middle-aged man with a German rasp. "A novice stumbling upon some artifact or device might show such a spike in the currents of magic, but this source feels organic. How could it appear out of nowhere and at such strength? Where is the gradual build-up one would expect from a language's practice?"

They all turned to the fourth member, Patrice Wu, who had traveled the farthest and been the last to arrive.

"I have reviewed the contents of every collection and warehouse—every magical artifact we own or monitor. With the exception of the furor caused by the necromancer Iosefa Malifa and the reappearance of several portions of the *Demon Codex*, nothing is amiss. I asked the Librarian to call a meeting because I am concerned that in America, Derrick Watson is showing signs of being the Scorpion. I want to be sure."

"The Scorpion is a myth," insisted the Cataloger, sweeping his hand before him as if, by doing so, he could dismiss all discussion.

The Custodian ignored the gesture. "Myth or prophecy, concern about the Scorpion is why the Folio was formed. Our purpose has never been to track and defend against the obvious threats to magic but to stand ready when a powerful and previously benign mage reveals their true nature. Humanity has produced many ambitious and unscrupulous men over the centuries, including magic users. It is inevitable that another will appear."

The Librarian raised a finger to capture their attention. "Set aside the question of Watson for the moment. I promise you we'll come back to it. This blip, this anomaly, has surfaced in much the same place as Malifa's recent activity. Surely that is no coincidence."

The Curator cleared his throat. "Even if I were inclined to believe in coincidences, there is another event that would suggest there is something more."

"Related to this surge in magic energy?"

"No, related to a fragment of the *Demon Codex*. Thirty years ago, I was responsible for recovering and re-hiding one piece of it. At the time, I crafted a map and passed it to my apprentice so he could find the pages if I became unavailable and there was need. He died and took the knowledge of that map with him to the grave. Recently, I have had conflicting reports that the map has surfaced, either in whole or in part."

"You think Malifa is seeking more pieces of the book?" The Cataloger's concern came with a gasp.

"Impossible. Malifa is dead," assured the Librarian.

Wu, the Custodian, drummed her fingers on the table. "When I spoke to Watson, he suggested Malifa might have…transcended death."

"I would not trust the death of any necromancer, least of all one as accomplished as Malifa," agreed the Curator. "And that was before he had sought out other portions of the *Codex*. I was on my way to reclaim the fragment that had been entrusted into my care so I could again hide it when I detoured to answer the summons and come here."

"I fear our Custodian is correct in general, if not specifically," responded the Librarian. "We are approaching the type of event that necessitated the creation of our society."

"You think that signals the arrival of the Scorpion?" asked the Cataloger. "Surely that conclusion is premature."

The Librarian stepped away from the others but paused in front of the room's windows as if the streaks of rain held answers beyond what might be found within. "Derrick Watson has long been on our watch list as a candidate, someone with the *potential* to become the Scorpion. His closest friend and most powerful colleague, Iosefa Malifa, has not only perfected the creation of soul bottles but also demonstrated a hunger for pieces of the *Demon Codex*. More, he apparently satisfied that appetite on multiple occasions. Now, a new source of power has been detected in the vicinity of both men. I dislike coincidences, and more so when they begin piling up."

The Curator sighed. "You want me to go to America and investigate directly, don't you?"

The Librarian turned to face him. "I do, but first, finish the task our gathering interrupted. Even if Watson is on his way to becoming the Scorpion, there should be sufficient time to relocate your fragment before you need to assess his situation."

"And if, in my judgment, Derrick Watson is indeed growing into the mantle of the Scorpion?"

The other three silently exchanged glances.

The Custodian responded. "In preparation for the possibility, even though I owe him for my training and my life, I will prepare and provide whatever tools you need to eliminate the threat he poses while we still can."

"And if I err in my assessment?"

"Then you will have killed an innocent man, and we will all mourn his loss. Even so, we cannot risk the arrival of the Scorpion in the world. I would see a hundred like Watson die before we allow the prophecy to come to fruition."

The Librarian silently stretched a hand to the middle of the table. "Are we agreed?"

Three hands joined hers.

CHAPTER FOURTEEN

<u>Albert's Apartment</u>

Letters, glyphs, and sigils danced in the air of Albert's studio. Green for 'ry. Red for Mem. Blue, purple, and yellow for bits and pieces of other demonic languages. They had started off clear and distinct, but he had cut them into syllabic pieces, rearranging and weaving them in parallel strands that pushed the limits of grammatical acceptability. None of them went over the edge, though some came close, and others extended and teetered just short of plunging to a lexical doom.

Hold still.

Albert infused more Will as he spliced the words that hung around him, blending phrases from the various languages into the slots he'd created using Centzontōtōchtin grammar.

Why is my hand shaking?

More Will. More concentration. Another phrase completed.

That works. Yeah, I just need to find a way to finish the phrase.

Sweat ran down his neck as the words comprising the spell grew in size and complexity. The room shone with a kaleidoscope of magical light.

The Maxwell. The answer is in there. I don't need much. I just need to juxtapose a basic morpheme so it lines up with the syntax and then force it into the formula.

Something throbbed behind his right eye. A moment later, it stabbed him and forced him to lift a hand to rub at it.

WAAAAAAA!

An air raid siren went off inside the room.

He lost his focus and the magical runes disappeared, plunging the room into shadow. The light from his cellphone shone from the floor as Albert fell to his knees in exhaustion.

"Dammit!"

Something blocked the glow of the phone for an instant, and the siren stopped wailing. He sighed with relief.

"What the hell? It felt like my ears were going to start bleeding."

Tiny paws raced across his leg, up his torso, over his chest, and eventually gently rubbed his cheek. He blinked and turned his head to find H.H. perched on his shoulder, the imp gently moving a paw against the mage's stubble.

"Are you okay, Albert?"

"Yeah. Mostly. What in God's name was that noise?"

"I triggered an app I'd installed on your phone. It's a blend of Basque ambulance sirens, time-compressed metal fatigue from the implosion of a skyscraper, and the wail of a banshee."

"Why would you put that on my phone?"

"You weren't looking too good. I thought you might have become stuck in there." The imp poked the side of Albert's head like someone knocking on a piece of wooden furniture for good luck. "So, I brought you out in the most expeditious way."

Albert rolled his head and worked his jaw. Everything still seemed to be in place. "Thanks. I think."

His familiar shrugged and dropped back to his shoulder, then scampered down his body and leapt to the floor. "Don't sweat it. My fate is tied to yours, so helping you is self-interest on my part. It's not as though I like you or anything."

Albert stood up and wobbled. A combination of overworked exhaustion and ravenous appetite reminded him he'd been at things too long. He glanced across the apartment's open floor plan into the kitchen and the clock on the distant microwave.

"It's almost midnight? I started well before eleven o'clock. That's crazy. I can't believe I held my focus on the magic for that amount of time. I've never heard Professor Watson talk about doing anything for that long. It's not sustainable, not at that level of concentration."

"Humans can't handle that kind of thing. Not your bodies and not your brains. It's suicidal to try is what it is." H.H. scowled up at Albert from the floor. "You need to eat something. Now. Do you have any idea how much glucose you burned through in that time? Like a marathon runner, only concentrated."

"I wouldn't have thought so, but the way I feel now? Yeah, I can believe it."

"This is a bad idea," suggested H.H. "Maybe you should go back on your meds."

Albert crossed to the kitchen and opened the apartment's fridge, claiming the remaining two-thirds of a pizza from the night before. He didn't bother heating it, just tore a slice free, barely chewing each bite before swallowing it like a jaguar gulping down a fresh kill, if jaguars were into pepperoni and Italian sausage. That first slice sated his immediate hunger, allowing him to slow down. Only then did he pull the box out of the fridge. With his other hand, he grabbed a couple of bottles of beer and staggered back across the room to slump on the couch. He twisted the cap off one of the bottles and started on the next slice.

"That's not happening." Albert didn't say any more until he'd progressed halfway through the second slice and washed it down with a couple of swigs of beer. "I know you don't understand the human experience of working magic, but it's not something I'm giving up. I've only ever been able to manage the simplest of effects before now. This is...well, it's indescribable."

"Describing it won't matter if you wind up dead." H.H. joined him on the couch and sat on its hind legs. "You gonna eat all that pizza yourself or what?"

Albert finished most of his second piece and handed over the crust. It was the one food they could enjoy in a symbiotic way. H.H. was all about the dough and couldn't care less what toppings came with the pie.

The imp continued speaking through bites of crust. "Better no Will than ending up not being able to unlock your focus and pull out of the magic. What do you think would have happened to you if I hadn't snapped you out of it?"

Albert tossed back most of a beer and reached for another slice of pizza. He stopped before picking it up and stared at his familiar. "That's it!"

H.H. had torn the crust into bite-sized portions and held one between its paws, nibbling delicately. "What's it? That piece of pizza?"

"Piece, yes, but not of pizza. The piece I've been missing."

"You lost me, Al."

"You're too close to see it."

"Close? I'm right here. What are you talking about?"

"I'm talking about the replacement for my medications."

"You just said you don't want to go back on your meds."

"I don't need to. I've got you."

"Me?"

Albert reached for the slice again and took a big bite, grinning as he chewed. "What's the point of having a familiar if I don't take full advantage of you to work magic?"

"First off, don't call it 'taking advantage.' It makes me feel cheap. So, what, you want me to hit you with an alarm when you've gotten too deep into your mojo?"

"We'll come up with something better than that, but essentially, yes. If you can monitor me and yank my attention back to something else, I'll have the best of both worlds."

H.H. considered Albert's suggestion as it finished the bites of pizza crust. "What's in it for me?"

Albert grinned. "Well, for starters, if I get a good handle on working magic, I can finally graduate. You're always complaining about being stuck with me at the university and living in this boring neighborhood. Imagine where we might go if I could finally use what I've been studying all this time?"

"I want to go to Syria."

"Syria? Seriously? Why there? Do you not watch the news?"

The imp shrugged. "That's where hamsters come from. I think it would be a good place to visit."

He laughed. "Why not? I'm good with that. Syria it is, assuming this all works out and I remember to renew my Spanish passport."

"Deal. So, how about instead of an alarm to pull you back from your personal abyss, I climb up and bite down hard on your earlobe?"

CHAPTER FIFTEEN

Camden, New Jersey

Looking across the river at the city of Philadelphia, Cassandra recalled what she'd told Janice. She'd hinted at her role in making magic accessible. The world had been on the brink of disaster, with the US using the newest of the post-Dee demonic languages to advance physics in pursuit of weaponry of unrivaled destruction, then unleashed it. In the aftermath, her efforts with Everett suggested the end of the world was near, so she'd scoured parallel timelines, desperate to find an alternative to global destruction within the next few years.

The most viable solution had been absurd. It had existed in fewer than one out of a thousand alternate realities she could see. Unfortunately, no one had a better idea, not her counterparts in the Folio, who were caught up in their fear of prophecy, and certainly not the magic-eschewing members of Tornat. As unlikely as it was, she'd brought the possibility to her superiors, and wonder of wonders, they'd promoted her on the spot and put her in charge of saving the world.

. . .

Moonrise Diner, Arizona, 1945

At precisely 3pm, two men approached the diner from opposite ends of the parking lot, acknowledging one another with silent nods and entering through the glass doors together. The taller of the pair had an athletic build, a full head of blond hair, and a faded tan that suggested he had forgone leisure activity for some time but had once enjoyed the sun. The shorter man was older, stockier, and compensated for his growing baldness with a bristling mustache.

A hostess greeted them and asked if they preferred a booth or seats at the counter. Before either man could explain that they were there to meet someone, a man tucked into a far corner booth waved them over.

"Thank you both for coming," said the third as the new arrivals took seats on the bench opposite him. "Were either of you followed?"

The taller of the pair, Gunderson, looked confused and shrugged. Reynolds, the shorter man, just looked annoyed. "Of course we were followed," he stated in the tone one might use to acknowledge the sky was blue or water was wet. "That's a given. It's been less than three months since the bomb. I don't care how junior we are. It's gonna be a long time before any of us can go anywhere without being followed."

"But you weren't detained?" pressed the third man.

"No, Captain," Reynolds assured him. "It's all been hands-off so far."

Gunderson nodded in agreement but added nothing.

"Call me Red," insisted the captain. "I'm not in uniform, and this is *not* a military or governmental meeting."

"Not?" asked Reynolds. "I thought Grove had sanctioned everything."

Red nodded. "He did, and Oppie as well, though there's nothing official on the books. When we leave, I don't expect any of us to ever meet again."

Gunderson stirred. "Then how are we to accomplish anything?" The whine in his voice grated.

Before Red could reply, a woman seated at the counter slid off her stool and approached their table. "That's why I'm here."

All three men started. None could recall seeing anyone seated at the counter near their table when they'd arrived.

"Relax, gentlemen," she assured them. "And please, no need to get up. Captain, if you'd slide over a bit, I'll take a seat. We'll be less conspicuous that way." Red complied, and she settled into the booth alongside him.

"Who are you?" asked Reynolds.

"Why don't we hold off introductions until the last of our group arrives? I doubt it will be long, Mr. Reynolds."

"You know who I am? You know who we all are?"

She responded with a dazzling smile. She was quite attractive, probably early forties, her honey-blonde hair in a bun. In other circumstances, one or more of the men might have considered making a play, but that was not what they were there for. While they didn't yet have all of the details of why they'd assembled at a nondescript diner, they knew enough to know that.

"I'm the one who put this meeting together," she explained. "Oppie and I go way back. I'm sure he'd like to be involved much more directly, but he can't. His profile's too high."

"Too high for what?" asked Red.

Before she could answer, a man emerged from the restroom around the corner from the end of the counter. He grabbed a loose chair, carried it to their booth, braced the back of it against the outer edge of the table, and straddled it as he sat.

"For one thing, too high profile to meet with me," explained the newcomer.

"Who are you?" asked Reynolds.

"You can call me Number Five."

"Why, because you were the fifth to arrive?" asked Red. "Who sent you?"

"He's here to represent the Folio," explained the blonde woman. "He's their Librarian."

"I thought the Folio was a myth." Gunderson paused, then added, "A story to scare student practitioners."

"We work very hard to maintain that myth," replied Number Five. "But I assure you we're as real as Cassandra's organization." His nod indicated the blonde woman.

"Which is?" asked Reynolds.

"Péra." Then at their looks of confusion added, "It's Greek. It means 'beyond.'"

"Beyond what?" Reynolds again.

"We're tasked with much the same purpose as the Folio," she offered, "albeit with a more general focus."

"Which is?" Reynolds inquired, and the growl in his voice made it clear he didn't like having to ask twice.

"To keep magic from blowing up the world. That is why I arranged to have the three of you join us. Each of you was involved with the development of the atomic bomb, and you know that more than physics and engineering went into its creation. You're all aware that some of the intel we received from the British in '42 was in the form of metaphors and grammatical structures overheard by Aoede practitioners listening to whispers from the Maxwell plane."

"That's not in any report," stated Red.

Cassandra smiled again. "No, Captain, it's not. There's no paper trail, but—I know you'll find this delightfully ironic—people have talked about it to one another. People including you."

"My people," Number Five assured the table, "have some of the best Aoede practitioners on the planet."

"So, what's your game?" asked Red. "I can't believe Grove would sanction a clandestine meeting designed to blackmail us. If that's your intention, be advised that even before witnessing the actual power of the A-bomb, I'd have had no hesitation killing both these men and the two of you, then turning the gun on myself rather than risk information getting out."

"Relax, Captain. I applaud your common sense and patriotism. There are larger issues at stake, though. The Folio is in agreement with your sentiments. That is why, along with Cassandra's organization, we concocted a scheme to lessen the likelihood anyone else can use Aoede to gain the name of a Maxwell demon. If humanity intends to build more bombs, they're going to have to rely solely on physics."

"No magic?" asked Gunderson. The whiny tone in his voice had vanished, replaced by hope.

"That's the goal," assured Number Five.

"It's impossible." Reynolds' tone left no room for contradiction. "Now that we've seen an atomic bomb, anyone skilled in Aoede will have a better idea of what to listen for. The rhythms and sounds of Maxwell are very distinct."

"I don't disagree," replied Number Five. "The information is out there for anyone who knows how to listen. As you say, there are individuals with the ability to learn that demon's name."

"You're wasting our time." Reynolds glanced around the diner like a man who was ready to leave.

"Hear us out," requested Cassandra. "I think you'll find this solution to be quite simple. Elegant, really."

"Basically, it's a signal-to-noise problem," explained Number Five.

"Come again?" asked Red.

"The name of the Maxwell demon is out there, and we agree that an Aoede practitioner could discover it. Let me break the problem down further. The number of Maxwell speakers is small. As a direct consequence, the corpus of material that Aoede practitioners might search is likewise small, even against the backdrop of competing spoken phrases from other demonic languages that could muddy, or at least delay, successfully targeting the name of a Maxwell demon. That's the signal;

nothing we can do about it. There's no point in shutting that particular barn door since the demon's name is out there."

"Like I said, wasting our time," repeated Reynolds.

"Not at all. I said it was a signal-to-noise problem. The name's the signal. We can't take it back. What we *can* do is increase the noise and make it harder to detect that signal."

"How do you plan to do that?" asked Red.

Cassandra picked up the explanation. "Throughout history, the majority of humanity has been blissfully ignorant of the existence of magic. We propose to change that."

"How?" asked Red, the question coming out in a growl.

"Education," explained Cassandra. "In the next few months, a proposal will be made to select the leadership of the newly formed United Nations. We'll start slowly, but within a year, we'll have departments at major universities throughout the western world."

"What kind of departments? Departments for what?"

"Demonic languages," said Number Five. "Right now, we estimate there are fewer than one thousand speakers with fluency in one or more demonic languages and the Will to use that talent in the world. We tend to be isolated and work in secret. We rarely, if ever, confer with one another except in secretive gatherings, not unlike this one. We're going to change that. We're going to bring magic to the forefront."

Cassandra gestured at the men around the table. "Gentlemen, it is our intention to showcase magic's utility as we flood the world with spoken exercises and practice in unearthly languages."

Red nodded in understanding. "Right, which in turn will create more background noise for anyone using Aoede."

"That's the plan," agreed Number Five. "It won't prevent it, but as the noise level increases, only the most proficient Aoede practitioners will be able to cut through it."

"And the effort to do so," continued Cassandra, "will draw attention to itself."

"Only if you have people dedicated to watching for that," added Reynolds critically.

Cassandra smiled for the third time. "We've had a team in place for just that since Alamogordo."

"What do you need us for?" asked Gunderson.

Cassandra smiled at him. "Number Five and I want separate things from you. I'm asking each of you three to chair one of the new university departments and teach elementary Maxwell."

Reynolds frowned. "To create more noise against the signal you're trying to hide?"

"Exactly," replied Number Five. "An overall increase in demonic languages will be a great help. An increase specific to Maxwell will have a still greater effect."

"Aren't you worried that in the process of training new Maxwell practitioners, you'll create people with the abilities to magically create atomic bombs?" asked Reynolds.

"Or worse," added Red. "The same principles can be applied to the other areas of Maxwell. Have you considered that, Number Five? Time bombs? Gravity bombs? Things we don't have the physics for. Truly gifted practitioners could use the metaphors learned at Los Alamos to create such weapons."

"First, it's not our intention to teach Maxwell at such a high level," explained Cassandra. "And yes, before you say it, I know there will be those who nonetheless manage to take their studies to those heights, but that's always a concern. This way, we'll have the advantage of knowing who and where they are. We'll be tracking every student of the language. We won't be taken unaware."

"We're not pretending there isn't a risk," added Number Five. "Obviously, there is. Some of the best minds from the Folio and Péra looked at this situation from every angle, and we believe the benefits outweigh the dangers many times over. Right now, the greatest danger is not from a Maxwell practitioner but rather from an Aoede speaker rediscovering the name of a Maxwell demon.

"Our main objective is to bury the names."

"What if we need them one day?" asked Gunderson. "It might be hard to imagine in the aftermath of Hiroshima, but we don't know what the future will bring. What if there comes a time when we find ourselves in a spot that requires us to summon a Maxwell demon? Not for destruction, but for protection, for creation, for saving ourselves."

"That's where I come in," replied Cassandra. "I assume you're all familiar with *gli Anderlibri*?"

"What, first Greek and now Italian?" asked Gunderson.

"Actually, it's an extinct language related to Romagnol," explained Number Five.

"Another myth." Red scowled.

"Hardly that," replied Cassandra. "The fragments of the original book are very real. As we go forward on the education front to increase the signal-to-noise ratio, Péra wants to safeguard what has already been learned."

"You want to create a new piece of the *Demon Codex*?" asked Gunderson, his voice heavy with disbelief.

She nodded. "Moreover, I want the three of you to do it."

Red shook his head. "I know these gentlemen and their background better than they know themselves. None of us have the expertise to do that."

"No," agreed Cassandra, "but I do, and I will provide you with templates. The three of you possess the raw information to complete those templates. The Folio is in possession of Dee's formula to ensure that when you're finished, we'll have an indestructible record that will allow a Maxwell speaker—should the need ever arise—to summon a demon from that plane."

"What will you do with that once we've all done our part."

"We'll do what others have done for hundreds of years,"

explained Cassandra. "Since the original scattering. We'll hide it where no one will find it."

"That's a pretty tall order," said Reynolds. "Why do you think it will work?"

Cassandra cast a sideways glance at Number Five, who leaned back in his chair. His face lit with a satisfied grin.

"Do you know anyone who has found any of *gli Anderlibri?*" He inclined his head at Cassandra. "Their track record is damn good."

CHAPTER SIXTEEN

Keflavik, Iceland

Hoping to arrive at his next destination in better condition, Watson took a sleeping pill shortly after boarding the plane and managed a solid fourteen hours during his flight from Beijing to Frankfurt. He added a brief nap on the flight from there to Iceland. As a result, he felt almost human as he clomped out of the terminal to the Keflavik car rental office and finally to the parking garage where his assigned vehicle awaited him.

Watson's original choice had been a sturdy sedan, but after explaining to the clerk his intention to drive the Golden Circle and listening to warnings of loose gravel and damaged undercarriages, he upgraded to a sturdy German SUV. The mileage wouldn't be as good, but the gas tank was larger, so it balanced out. Armed with a complimentary map, he headed north along the eastern side of the island. This wasn't a vacation trip, and Watson had no intention of exploring the attractions the clerk had circled on the map. After a few hours, he turned off the highway and drove cross-country toward the edge of a massive glacier.

The terrain became rougher by the second, and he was forced

to stop short of his intended goal for fear that even the SUV would get stuck. He got out, donned the cold-weather gear he'd purchased after he left the airport, and set out on foot. He followed a path he barely remembered, but he was determined to make progress during the little daylight remaining.

The professor huffed and puffed in a fair imitation of a wolf intent on blowing away diminutive porcine architecture, a fanciful thought that made him wonder if he was getting enough oxygen. He approached the edge of a massive crevice in the ice and paused to catch his breath. The sun had almost set.

"I need to get back into the gym."

Darkness fell with astonishing speed, and the temperature dropped further. He fumbled with a protein bar he'd bought at an airport kiosk, unwilling to remove his gloves to make ripping open the wrapper easier. Eventually, he tore it open with his teeth and consumed the thing in three bites, chewing ferociously until he could swallow it. He hoped it would help.

"Guess I'd best get moving."

He looked at the northern sky and enjoyed the aurora playing there. The majesty of the lights warmed his soul, if not his body. That would have to do. He stepped to the edge of the narrow crevice and began to climb down.

Watson moved slowly but steadily, his way lit by the cool gleam of a pair of light bars strapped to his forearms. Ledges and handholds were plentiful, albeit slippery. The wall stretched to either side, and a similar surface lay a few feet behind him. It had been years since Watson had done any serious rock climbing, but the old reflexes returned quickly. His confidence grew as he discovered this was a skill set that fell into the category of things that were like riding a bike. Despite the exertion and the cold, he was enjoying himself.

That was why it was a shock and a surprise when he lost his righthand grip while reaching for a new hold with his left.

His stomach lurched, and his limbs flailed. He grabbed at the wall but failed to catch a hold. As he dropped, reaching for anything, his fingers slid off the ice. He tried to stop himself or slow his fall, but his head bounced off the opposite wall, stunning him. Somewhere along the way, he managed to smash both light bars. The darkness within the glacier was absolute as he fell.

Adrenaline kept him near the surface of consciousness, but it wasn't enough. He vaguely noted pain as his elbow smashed into a wall. His ears acknowledged the scraping and ripping that occurred as he bounced, but it didn't mean much as he continued his slide into the icy depths of the crevice.

Then he stopped. His body caught against something, and a roar echoed off the ice.

A roar? That wasn't right. His brain tried to put his senses back in order. He needed more air, so he took several deep, gasping breaths. The mental fog cleared, and though he hadn't noticed its absence, his sense of smell returned, registering a heavy, musty scent. It was the kind of odor that might be admired from a distance but was an assault at close range.

Watson's brain added other pieces one at a time. He was still bouncing but not falling, though his motion had a downslope feel as if he were perched on top of something big that was descending at a formidable pace. He tried not to gag as his understanding of the smell progressed from odor to stench. He recognized that his perch was more than just large; it was hairy as well. The air grew warmer. Either there was still no light, or his watering eyes refused to open; he couldn't tell which. Finally, his rescuer reached level ground and slowed to a calmer pace. A glimmer of light shone in the distance, and as Watson drew nearer, the professor realized he was in a tunnel. He rounded a bend and the light expanded, filling his surroundings. He was set down on something soft and comfortable, where he collapsed like a discarded Muppet, his limbs limp and rubbery. Over the course of several minutes, using his fingertips to drag them, he worked his arms up across his torso and gently placed his fingers against his head. They came away sticky with blood.

"Ouch."

Watson winced, which, oddly, helped him focus. He looked around and discovered he was in a large ice cave. It was decorated like a suburban husband's man-cave, complete with black furniture and an early model flat screen tv. A soccer game was on.

Sounds came from his left, and Watson gingerly turned his head in that direction. He saw a massive back covered in dingy fur. It may have looked white in the right lighting, but it looked like matted, dirty slush to Watson.

There was no debate. He stared at the house-sized backside of the legendary abominable snowman, a yeti out of myth.

Watson finally caught his breath and looked away. Feeling had returned to his arms and he took a moment to wipe the blood off his hands onto his sleeves. By reflex, he ran his fingers through his hair as if that would resolve any lack in his appearance. The familiarity of the movement calmed him.

His brain went back into operation, and the panic and adrenaline produced by his fall subsided. As his heart rate slowed, he noticed the cave was warm—so much so that he unzipped his parka and unwound his scarf. He pulled off first one glove, then the other, keeping his gaze locked on the maze of knots in the handmade rug in front of him. He tried to make sense of its pattern but decided it didn't have one.

A cross between an impatient grunt and the backfire of Trixie's old truck finally brought his head back up, and he locked eyes with the yeti. They were bright and yellow and full of intelligence.

Watson spoke first. "Hello, Aron. You're looking well. I've come about the pages you've been holding onto."

CHAPTER SEVENTEEN

<u>Alexander University, Philadelphia</u>

Albert slumped in his chair. His arms hung limp at his sides, and his feet, which had been propped up on the edge of his desk, splayed to either side. His eyes glazed over as he stared into space at something only he could see. Nearby, H.H. sat atop its hamster house, building a small stack of gold coins. It pulled them one at a time from within its voluminous cheeks while considering the human.

"You're wasting time." H.H. pulled another coin out of its mouth, tiny paws struggling to get it free and add it to the stack.

"I'm working," Albert murmured, the words emerging from his slack mouth at half speed and devoid of inflection.

"You're dithering."

Albert stirred. He planted his feet firmly on the floor, then sat up and rubbed his eyes. "I've spent the last eight years studying a dozen languages from other realms of existence. I'm trying to decide what to use from which of them."

"Yeah, that's not going to work for you."

"Why not? I've got adequate fluency in most of them, and now that I have access to my Will, I'm more than motivated enough to bring my skills up in the few where I need more work."

"That would require a lot of focus."

Albert grinned. "Focus is one thing I have in spades!"

H.H. withdrew another coin from its mouth like a magician pulling objects out of a hat. "Sure, your ADHD is great for that once you lock in on something, but you're going to suck at switching back and forth between languages. Your precious focus is going to work against you and cause you to get stuck. You'll be worse off than you were before you started.

"Instead, just pick one. Do it now. I'm not saying you need to specialize like most human mages, but you do need to start with a foundation in one language. You can always embellish it with spells drawn on magical energies from other realms after you've built your base."

"You have a point, but which language?"

"I don't know from grammar, only that the languages all have different ones. Are some easier for you or easier for your ADHD issues?"

"Stanley made a good argument for working with an agglutinative language."

"A gluten language? Are you speaking it or eating it? Is bread magic a thing?"

"Not gluten, 'agglutinative.' It's a linguistic classification that applies to some languages."

"Oh. Sorry." The hamster hacked up another coin. "I have no idea what that means."

"It's what we discussed at the farm. You build words by stringing together bits of meaning, or morphemes."

"Morphine? You're going to get into drugs now?"

Albert glared at his familiar, unsure if the imp was being deliberately obtuse. "Not morphine, 'morphemes.' Linguistic pieces of meaning. English doesn't use a lot of them but think about how adding an 's' to most nouns makes them plural. That's a morpheme. Some languages have thousands of morphemes. That's what Stanley was talking about when he told me he could build a spell and alter it by swapping out tiny pieces. Morphemes are the pieces, and a syntax heavy in them would work well with my ADHD."

"Well, there you go. Which magical languages you've studied do this A-gluten thing?"

"Again, not gluten, agglutinative. Weren't you listening when I talked about this with Trixie?"

"Hey, you of all people don't get to lecture me about paying attention, okay?"

"Fine. So, Maxwell, obviously, but I'm not as proficient in that as I'd need to be."

"Okay, so scratch that one. What else?"

"Mem."

"The water elemental language? That worked so well for Jason Holloway."

"Um, yeah. Well, there's also Centzontōtōchtin, and I've got a certain proficiency there. You remember the demo I did for Trixie? It was a good illustration that I have Will, but I don't see that as being very useful."

"The drunk divine rabbit language?"

Albert tried and failed to suppress a grin. "It's the language of illusion and hallucination."

"Sounds perfect?"

"It doesn't really *do* anything. It's all façade and fakery."

"Is it?"

"What do you mean?"

"Do you know of any humans who have really pushed it? Taken it to the level Stanley has with Maxwell? Built bigger and bigger spells?"

"Well, no. Not that we know of. I mean, who are we going to ask? I might be the first person to seriously pursue it since the conquistadors arrived. What's the point?"

"Trust me on this. I'm an imp who's stuck in your realm in the guise of a golden hamster. You humans are constantly being deceived by your senses. What you perceive determines what you believe. Illusion is huge. You should start working on spells using those drunk bunnies." H.H. gagged as it pulled an especially large coin out of its cheek pouch, causing Albert to sit up and notice the growing pile of coins on his desk.

"What are you doing?"

"Building your nest egg."

"What?"

"Once you figure out what magic you want to use, you're going to have expenses."

"I have money. I'm what Americans call a trust fund boy, remember?"

"Sure, but it's all tied to accounts with your name on them."

"So?"

"Trust me on this, Trust Fund Boy. I've had several of your lifetimes to learn that when you're making a major change, keeping as much of it as secret as possible is never a bad idea."

"So, if I've got this right, you're advocating not only illusion but secrecy for me?"

"Think it through, Albert. You've just discovered you're a mage with more potential power than most practitioners with twice your years. Not everyone is as benign as Watson. Some people don't react well to others possessing power. You need to protect yourself."

"From what?"

"That's just it," answered the familiar. "We don't know. Right now, the unknown is your biggest danger. So, build yourself some protections from the start."

Albert nodded. "You're saying, let Alberto Hernandez Alcaldo continue as he's been—the perennial grad student with no Will to use the skills he's worked at."

"Exactly."

"Hmm." Albert fell silent and closed his eyes. His face went slack, and his lips twitched. He raised one hand, and his fingers danced in the air as if he was tapping on bricks in a wall. After half an hour of this, during which time H.H. produced another two dozen gold coins, he dropped his hand and opened his eyes.

"You got something?" asked H.H.

"We'll see. Centzontōtōchtin's grammar does mesh nicely with my new focus." Before H.H. could say more, Albert spoke in another language. His delivery was calm and precise, as if he were reading or reciting from memory. It went on and on in a rhythm unlike any human language, though most of the sounds were found in English. After ten minutes, he finished and exhaled a sigh before slumping in his chair.

H.H. waited for a moment, rearranging his coins into several stacks. "What's the illusion? I don't see anything. Nothing's happened."

"Oh, it happened," replied Albert. "I've hung the spell, using the technique Stanley suggested. I haven't triggered it yet, but the hard part is done, so I can access it any time."

"Great. Let's see it."

"I took your suggestion to heart. I don't want anyone to know what I can do. Unlike the stuff I showed Trixie, I'm not simply copying the appearance of others. I've created a completely new illusion: an alternate identity, like a magical pseudonym."

"You look the same to me."

"Wait for it." Albert smiled and stood. An instant later, he vanished and was replaced by an older figure, taller and leaner, with long, gleaming black hair and deep-set green eyes. He might have been Alberto's really attractive cousin, but nobody would mistake him for the same man. He was clothed in a dark suit that seemed to swallow the light, impeccably tailored and pressed. When he spoke, his voice was deeper, and his Spanish accent was much more pronounced. "Behold Asombro, master magician." He held out a hand and a trio of salamanders danced upon his palm, their flames leaping.

"You've gotten much better at using 'ry," noted H.H. "Even more impressive while using illusion magic."

"The salamanders are part of the illusion," explained Albert/Asombro. "But it's guided by my knowledge of 'ry, giving it an extra edge of realism. As far as anybody else is concerned, Asombro is a master of elemental magic."

"Nice," acknowledged H.H. "Misdirection is your friend. You're going to be fine, kid. Now, let's discuss what this Asombro fellow is going to do and what other kinds of spells you need to work on while your focus is still sharp."

CHAPTER EIGHTEEN

Petra, Jordan

The Gliman sat in the back of the service taxi and dozed. Her Bedouin driver maintained a running commentary, ranging from current events to popular tourist destinations to solutions to the local economy and the vagaries of the weather. She'd put up with worse. His chatter was amiable, and his heavily accented English was made more palatable by the pleasant timbre of his voice. Best of all, he didn't require a response from her, seeming quite pleased to prattle on as long as she didn't object. The arrangement allowed her to drift, never quite falling asleep as the car bounced along on the road from Amman to the ancient Nabataean city of Petra in the south of the country.

The sun hadn't risen yet, and if things went according to plan, she'd arrive before it did.

"We are very close, Miss. Three kilometers. Abdallah will have you there in a minute."

"That's great. *Shukran*." She glanced up to meet his gaze in the taxi's rearview mirror. *The way you drive, we'll be there in seconds.*

Sure enough, roughly a minute later, the car pulled into an

empty lot near the sandstone cliffs that surrounded Petra. The Gliman handed over the agreed-upon fare plus a generous tip that was politely refused, but only once. Abdallah graciously accepted it on her second offer. She'd never had any doubt that he would.

Dawn arrived, and within minutes, the first tour buses pulled into the lot. Gaggles of European and Chinese tourists poured out and formed up in clusters under brightly colored umbrellas wielded by loud and insistent tour guides. The Gliman shuddered, imagining each guide droning on in condescending nasal tones.

Ahead of her, a cut in the cliffs loomed large, yawning wide as the only path into the ancient city. The sight was iconic, but for all the wrong reasons. Everyone knew it as the path Indiana Jones took to the temple in the *Last Crusade*. Here it was called the *Siq*.

Not that the Gliman had any intention of entering the city. Her quarry lay outside its walls. To that end, she pulled a map fragment from her pocket and studied the worn and painted cloth. Glancing up, she surveyed the shadowed rocks and mounds and quickly found what she was looking for: the Djinn blocks.

Each block stood several stories tall. They lined the path to the Siq like squat red stone guardians. They were sometimes called God blocks, but not much was known about them. They dated to sometime around the first century BCE, and even from a distance, the Gliman couldn't help but notice the area all but hummed with unspent magical energy.

The Gliman folded her map and slowly drifted in the direction of the blocks. As the tour groups began to move, she casually followed, straggling behind. When the moment presented itself, she made her way around the first of the monoliths. Confident that nobody had noticed her, she stepped into the shadows between a block and the cliff face. She paused and listened for another moment, then projected her Will into a well-rehearsed Maxwell spell and leapt into the air. Her magic lifted her and propelled her swiftly and silently to a recess in the cliffs adjacent to a Djinn block.

She peeked out, double-checking that no one had seen her, but there were no frantically pointing tourists below, just a well-ordered line approaching the Siq. Satisfied, the Gliman settled into her hiding place and prepared for the long day ahead.

Around nine o'clock, she stripped off her leather jacket. She'd consumed one of her three water bottles and the temperature was rising quickly, even in her shadowy spot.

The hours ticked by, hot and sweaty. The Gliman read the trashy paperback she'd brought along and snacked on trail mix. In general, she tried very hard not to engage in physical activity.

By the time the sweat trickling down the back of her pants threatened to drive her crazy, the sun dipped on the western horizon, and the temperature plunged along with it. The lingering sweat on her skin cooled her, which was a welcome relief at first, but then a chill set in, so she retrieved her jacket. She nibbled her final bits of granola and listened to the last of the tour buses departing for the day.

"About time," she muttered.

Another hour passed and the stars appeared, filling the sky with brilliant pinpoints of light. The Gliman continued to wait, and eventually, her patience was rewarded. Sensing that she was no longer alone, she rolled slowly to the edge of her hiding place and looked down.

Two men, one in his late fifties and another who was much younger, stood at the base of the block, barely visible by starlight. They were as out of place as she was, and they proved that point by looking right at her.

"You'll pardon my saying so, but you don't belong here," stated the older of the pair.

"Judging by your accent, I think the same could be said of you. Or has Jordan begun selling archaeological real estate to Germany?"

A chuckle rose in the darkness. The second figure whispered, "Why is she here?" The whisperer sounded Slavic to her ear.

"In this place and time? Probably for the same reason we are, Oleg. She knows that when the stars align tonight, the block will open. She's come to attempt to claim the prize for herself."

"Not so much," replied the Gliman. "I'm here to make sure it doesn't fall into the wrong hands."

"We're not the wrong hands," asserted Oleg. "Do you even know what's here?"

He sounded so young and earnest that the Gliman couldn't help but smile. "If my sources are right, it's the Dushara piece of the *Demon Codex*."

"How would you know that?" asked the first voice.

"I have a map," she answered. "Well, half a map, but it was enough to get me here and let me deduce the rest."

"And the person with the other half?"

"I'm hoping he hasn't figured it out, or if he does, it won't be until after I've slipped away with the prize and denied him. So, please understand, it's nothing personal, but to ensure he doesn't get it, I have to keep you from taking it either. How is it you know anything about it?"

"I put it here," explained the German voice.

"What?"

"Thirty years past. A safe place, hiding a Dushara tool in plain sight."

"Clever."

"Thank you, but it would appear this spot is no longer safe. My intention is to move it, and with luck, gain another few decades. I created that map for my protégé, who was charged with safeguarding the pages after my passing. The universe had other plans and he predeceased me—a random traffic accident—

and the knowledge of the map passed from the living world with him."

The polite conversation was all well and good but beside the point. The Gliman began pulling up the mnemonic triggers that would give her swift access to the offensive and defensive magic she had developed, an assortment of rapid-fire cantrips and more elaborate spells. "How do you happen to be here now?"

"His grave was disturbed. Defiled, really, or so it was made to appear. I suppose it could also be evidence that a necromancer pulled him back to learn about the pages, which in turn led him to learn where to find the map."

"Malifa," replied the Gliman.

"Ah. Do you truly think so?"

"Who is Malifa?" asked Oleg.

"One of the most powerful speakers of Balaṭu of this century. I had heard he perished recently."

"I did," offered a new voice, "but I assure you, it's been little impediment. Even so, you really should be careful when invoking a name." The words came from a skeleton that stood a short distance from the other men. Emerald light shone from the depths of its eye sockets. Behind it lay the glowing portal it had stepped through.

"You are Iosefa Malifa?"

"I was, though the dead have little use for names. Now, I simply am. I've come to claim another of *gli Anderlibri* for my own uses."

The Gliman moved swiftly, letting her earlier spell propel her across the gap to land atop the Djinn block. Below, Oleg and the older man quickly moved apart as Malifa's skeleton stepped onto the sand and stone and closed the portal behind him.

Oleg shouted the trigger of a spell in a language the Gliman didn't recognize but whose magical effects were anything but subtle. Wind whipped across the terrain and rocks as big as fists pelted the lich, driving it backward through sheer savagery.

So that's what Dushara sounds like, she thought. *A language of wind and stone.*

CHAPTER NINETEEN

<u>**Liberty Place Mall, Philadelphia**</u>

Albert sat in a posh high-backed wicker chair alongside a glass and chrome table and watched shoppers go about decorating themselves with the latest styles. He sipped an espresso and reached for a biscotti from a plate on the table.

"I used to love fashion."

H.H. looked up from its biscotti and took a break from nibbling to respond with all the sarcasm a hell hamster could muster. "You don't anymore? That news will come as a shock to the three closets that house your clothes, plus the pair of dressers. Also the armoire—"

"Stop. I get it. I have a lot of clothes. Maybe too many clothes, but that's not what I mean."

H.H. resumed its nibbling, only to pause again and inquire, "What *are* you trying to say?"

"I'm trying to say it doesn't seem important anymore. Not since Fat Mage. Not since I got my magic back."

"Not since you stopped taking your medications."

"Sure, that too. I guess."

"Stop guessing, Al. You went through a traumatic experience, then you stopped taking the medications that had helped you cope and focus for decades. That, in turn, required you to cope with withdrawal. It only makes sense that your brain is going to toss you all sorts of odd thoughts and strange feelings and who knows what other bits of wonky stuff as it rewires itself."

Albert nodded. "I suppose you are right."

"Look, I'm your familiar, okay? Well, one of the things that goes with that job is that I can't help but care about your well-being. I wish I knew who had the bright idea of locking my kind into this sort of magical codependency. I'd strangle 'em and post it as a video on social media. Guaranteed to go viral. Until I get that chance, I'll look out for you. I know that your strange little human brain is going through some major weirdness right now. It's like the weather."

"The weather?"

"Yeah. You can complain about it, but that won't change it. Instead, let's focus on something productive."

"Like what?"

"Let's talk about that. Even though I still don't fully support your decision to stop taking your medications, it's what you chose to do, and you did it for a reason."

Albert sat up straighter. "Yeah, I did."

"What was that reason?"

"To see if I could find my Will. To see what magic I'm capable of."

"Bullshit. Stop lying to yourself, and don't start lying to me."

"I'm sorry?"

"Those aren't reasons. Those are just things. Means to an end. You need to step back and ask the larger question. What is your purpose, Albert? What is bigger than you? That's the thing that drives you. Can you articulate it? Put a name to it?"

The young mage rubbed his chin. "I want to help people."

"Which people?"

"Well, anyone."

"Anyone specific?"

Albert took another sip of his espresso. "Yeah. I want to help my friends. I want to help the people I love. I want to...keep them safe."

H.H. nodded its little hamster head. "Now we're getting somewhere. Any thoughts about how you're going to do that?"

Albert chuckled. "Sure. I have many. I have them constantly, but..."

H.H. listened intently as Albert's voice trailed off. The familiar waited for him to resume speaking, and when he didn't, it scurried across the glass tabletop and leapt onto Albert's arm. Then it raced up his shirtsleeve and around his collar to paw Albert's face. "Yes?"

Albert responded by plucking his familiar off his shoulder and set it back on the table. He leaned forward, scanning the sea of faces going by. A moment later, his face was replaced by that of a nearby security guard.

"I'm not sure..."

"Right. What does that tell you?" The imp knew better than to push the mage too far, too fast. It returned to its biscotti, its work done for now.

Albert dropped the illusion. He'd been doing face swaps for days. It was too easy. Too...little.

I need to up my game.

A moment later, the Spaniard took on the appearance of another passerby, but this time, he did more than replace his good looks. He also traded his curated outfit for a baggy pair of jeans and a dingy gray sweatshirt, rendering himself a duplicate of the acne-scarred adolescent boy who had just passed.

The imp looked him over, then scanned the crowd until he found the original. "You nailed it. The whole thing. Aren't you afraid he'll see you and freak out?"

"He's fifteen and walking past a Victoria's Secret store. He doesn't see anything but pictures of boobs."

"Humans are so predictable, even to one another."

"It's still not enough." Albert sighed as he dropped the illusion. "If I'm going to defeat Malifa—"

"Whoa! Al, slow your roll, buddy. Defeat a lich? You? I love you, man. I believe in you. You've demonstrated that you're capable of some pretty impressive stuff, with the potential for more. Now, get that idea out of your head, okay? You can't fight a lich. Malifa will demolish you."

Albert nodded. "You're right. *I* can't fight him. Not head-on, but maybe I don't have to."

"What do you mean?"

"Close your eyes for a second."

"Um, okay, but keep your hands off my biscotti."

Albert's eyes lost focus as he pulled on his Will. A moment later, he turned his attention back to the imp. "Okay, open them."

H.H. complied and looked nonplused when he saw Al standing ten feet away from the table. "Well, that was nothing."

A second later, the imp all but leapt out of its skin when the invisible Albert, who was still sitting in his chair, reached over and flicked the lesser demon's ear.

Albert dropped the invisibility spell and the mirror image of himself a moment later.

"What about that?"

H.H. rubbed its ear. "Was flicking my ear necessary?"

"No." Albert smirked. "Answer my question."

"Okay. I agree; it adds a new level of difficulty and complexity. I'd even go so far as to say it offers you more options in terms of defense than offense."

"When facing an enemy as powerful as Malifa, isn't that important?"

"Very," the imp agreed.

"Even a lich has a limited amount of Will, correct?"

H.H. scratched its furry head. "Theoretically. It's not like we have a lot of data available for comparison. Yes, I see where you are going with this. You could get Malifa to waste his Will and burn through the magic available to him by chasing shadows and illusions, but that kind of trick won't let you destroy him, and nothing short of total physical destruction is going to stop him."

"I know that, but if I could deplete his reserves, I could then unleash elemental magic to destroy him at my leisure."

"Leisure? Do you hear yourself? Have you been listening to me at all? He's a lich! You're not going to have any *leisure*, Al. You sure as heck won't know when he's out of juice. Also, nobody knows what it takes to destroy a lich. We don't even know if he can be taken out on this plane or if he has to be defeated in one of the necromantic realms. Oh, and newsflash: most of the necromantic realms are deadly for humans."

Al waved a hand dismissively. "You know what else is deadly? Sitting around and doing nothing."

"But you aren't. Watson's out there working against Malifa. He's connected to lots of magical talent, so I suspect he's not doing it alone, either. Also, he's been studying demonic languages for longer than you've been alive. You just got access to your Will. You're very new at this. Even if you weren't, how would you even go about finding Malifa?"

Al smiled. "I'm not going to find him. He's going to find me."

"Why would he want to find *you?*"

"Well, not me, but he *will* want to find Asombro, the master of the elements and the arcane." He extended his arms in a looping flourish and executed a seated bow.

When Albert sat back up, his face and outfit had been replaced by the powerful features and black ensemble of his new alter-ego Asombro.

The imp nodded slowly, its biscotti forgotten. "You might be right, Al. In fact, I'm afraid you are."

CHAPTER TWENTY

Seizing the opportunity, the Gliman scanned the top of the block, looking for evidence of an opening or some sign of the hiding place in which the Codex fragment had been hidden. Her eyes swept back and forth in vain until the stars quite literally aligned. A glamour several feet from her shimmered, and the barrier it had covered dissolved.

"Gotcha!" She dashed across the top of the Djinn block, her ears registering the sounds of the magical battle below. From the edges of her vision, she caught flashes of magical light that, coupled with the deafening bellow of the wind, meant the two strangers were holding their own.

Keep it up, boys.

The Gliman fell to her knees and examined the rock surface from which the illusion had faded. The last bits of the magical shield beneath it were giving way to the starlight. Precious seconds ticked by. The howl of the wind lessened but did not cease, suggesting the arcane combat was nearing an end. Even against two-to-one odds, she had little doubt that Malifa would emerge victorious.

"Come on!"

The barrier dissipated at last like a draining pool of silvery water.

"Dammit!" Retrieving the fragment was not going to be easy. The German guy, whoever he was, knew his stuff, and had protected it with more than a Centzontōtōchtin illusion and an Euskal shield.

A metal box covered with runes was set into the top of the Djinn block, perfectly aligned with its surface. She recognized the script of the runes, a commonplace alphabet for scrawling in what Watson had called Pre-Industrial imp back in her graduate days. The language was employed by the annoying denizens of a neighboring realm where everyone had a little bit of magic and precious little sense. Imps, when they manifested on Earth, acted like cartoon characters. They attracted trouble, fomented confusion, and made things explode. Case in point, the runes on the box indicated a detonation spell with a hair trigger. Anyone who tried to remove the box from the Djinn block would pull back a stump, assuming they didn't blow themselves to bits.

"I don't have time for this," she muttered as her eyes worked to unlock the puzzle. There had to be a way to disarm the damn thing. The Gliman was a specialist, and while she might recognize the language involved in the trap, she didn't know enough to read it or see the intention of whoever had crafted the runes—likely the German guy Malifa was beating up on—which might have offered a hint to defuse the magical bomb. She shrugged and stepped back.

"Not the way I would have chosen to go about this," she whispered as she dropped to her belly a few feet away. Then she placed her right palm flat against the stone surface of the block and pushed her Will into the archaeological treasure. "I'm really sorry." She winced.

For a moment, nothing happened. Then a five-foot section of rock erupted upward with devastating force. Shards and pebbles filled the sky as a directed explosion propelled them and the metallic box, into the air.

The Gliman jumped to her feet. Her eyes tracked the box. Her use of Will had done more than hurtle the box into the air. She had sprung its traps, unleashing arcs of magical electricity and flame as it rose above her. The Pre-Industrial Imp runes had contained more than an explosive. The bomb's creator had hidden other triggers in 'ry and Maxwell underneath as further protection. If the concussive force of the initial explosion didn't kill you, the blaze of a fireball or lightning strike would do the job.

I'm glad I didn't try to open it.

She leapt off the top of the Djinn block and used her mastery of Maxwell to fly in pursuit of the *Codex* piece.

Oleg knew they were in trouble. He'd prepared his most dangerous spell in case something went wrong, and something had—in a spectacular fashion.

The woman, no doubt a mage, had been an unwelcome but not unanticipated surprise. The presence of the lich, however, spelled disaster.

We must not let him get the Codex.

Uttering a simple phrase in Dushara coupled with a blast of Will, Oleg sent every rock and loose stone within thirty meters hurtling toward Malifa at a withering velocity after the lich emerged from its portal. It was very rocky terrain.

Malifa held up both bony hands and summoned a shield, but it was insufficient. The undead monster was driven to its knee bones by the ferocity of Oleg's assault. Deprived of the necromancer's focus, the portal that had delivered the lich to Petra crackled once, then collapsed in on itself.

As the projectiles continued their pummeling rain, Oleg

moved his hands in a series of well-rehearsed patterns to further focus his Will. Weaving complicated gestures like an orchestra conductor, he directed his projectiles into a vortex centered on the necromancer. Wind, sand, and stone buffeted the lich from every side, scouring its skeleton with abandon and grinding away at the enchanted bones.

The young mage glanced at his mentor, the Curator. "I don't know how long I can keep him like this. Get the *Codex*!"

The Curator nodded and moved to comply. The younger mage had his priorities in place but hadn't thought things through. It wouldn't be enough to obtain this fragment of *gli Anderlibri*. One of the two of them had to escape with it. The other would likely be sacrificed to the effort. The question of who would pay that price was rendered moot by an explosion.

The blast had come from atop the Djinn block. The Curator didn't doubt that the Gliman had caused the monolith to erupt, jettisoning the treasure from the hiding place into which he'd set it all those years before. He looked at the sky in shock as the American woman, clad in jeans and a leather jacket, streaked into the air amidst a cloud of debris. Ahead of her, glinting in the moonlight, the Pandora Box, an arcane creation of his own design, was tumbling upward with the force of the explosion.

When the box reached its zenith and slowed, the woman closed on it. She was twenty meters away. Ten. She reached toward the box.

The Curator shot his Will at the box and felt it recognize him. It yearned to return to its creator and ignored momentum to eagerly change direction and rush down the instant he yanked it. It flew away from the American's outstretched fingers and headed for home like a lost puppy who heard its master's voice.

The woman cursed in a most unladylike fashion and swept around in an arc that sent her careening toward the ground. She glared at the Curator as if to suggest he had cheated her of her rightful prize.

The old German shrugged in mock apology.

The woman favored him with a grin as she accelerated after the box.

"Son of a..." the Gliman spat as she was forced to reverse course to chase the box that held her goal.

As she reoriented toward the ground and the rapidly receding box, the old mage looked up at her and shrugged.

Did that old man just wink at me?

The Gliman chuckled at the mage's chutzpah. The geezer had tricks up his proverbial sleeve, and in other circumstances, she'd have bought him a drink and been delighted to talk shop for hours. Like her, he had clearly taken his general knowledge of an area of magic and refined one or more spells into something no one else possessed. He had snatched the box with the *Codex* fragment out of the air in a heartbeat. That kind of precision was difficult under the best of circumstances, and having your target moving at hundreds of miles an hour hardly qualified as optimum.

Who are you?

It didn't matter. The Gliman had two priorities. First, get the *Codex* piece. Second, if possible, take out Malifa. If the old guy got in the way, she'd deal with him. He was a grown-ass man and then some who clearly knew what was at stake and had made his choices.

Her eyes cut to where Malifa was being held at bay. The young mage had a lot of power, but it couldn't last. Her mind flickered to the adage about old age and treachery winning over youth and skill. It was trite, but that didn't mean it wasn't true.

As she pursued the magic box, Malifa's skeleton clawed its way back to its feet.

Hold him as long as you can, kid.

The Gliman locked her eyes on the box containing the *Codex* fragment.

It flew into the older man's hands as a blast of purple and green lightning struck the young mage.

The kid was thrown onto his back. The winds died instantly. The bombardment of rock and stone ended. A pile of debris had grown around Malifa, rising to near pelvis height, and while it had abraded the necromancer's bones, nearly wearing through several of them, the Gliman could see that since the attack had ended, fresh, ebony ossification was filling in the damage. Within minutes, it would be fully healed. Meanwhile, the lich pressed the heels of its former palms against the stones as it squirmed and sought to leverage itself free. It wouldn't take long.

The older mage tucked the box under one arm and raised the other toward the lich, who responded to the gesture by pausing its efforts and laughing.

Then Malifa raised its hands and summoned more lightning. The bolts danced around the necromancer for several seconds, eager servants heeding an inaudible call. Then they gathered together and lunged at the elder mage, lashing him like a series of magical whips. The lightning struck him from every angle, and Malifa returned its attention to pulling its skeletal body free of the cairn that pinned it in place, leaving the whips free to continue their attack with increasing ferocity.

But the German mage was no rookie. Before the first bolt reached him, his free hand danced through a pattern of movements to unleash a previously hung spell. A collection of indigo disks appeared in the air around him, further evidence of skill in Euskal. These shields darted about, interposing themselves between the mage and the lightning and absorbing the lich's magical strikes.

It was no stalemate, though. Malifa had only deployed the lightning as a delaying tactic while it freed itself from the stones. With that accomplished, it unleashed its full power.

Necromantic force leapt from the lich's extended hands. The number of lightning bolts doubled, and they rolled over the older mage with ever-increasing intensity. In response, more blue disks interposed themselves as shields, but each was smaller now, their color paler. Inevitability hung in the air.

He can't keep this up. The Gliman watched in growing disbelief.

She had prepared some magic in case she ran into Malifa again, though she wasn't sure how it would turn out. With a mental tug, she pulled into existence a spell that could, in theory, cause a piece of bone to collapse upon itself with the power of a *mostly* contained nuclear explosion.

There were only two small problems. First, she had to get close enough to place it. Second, having accomplished the first, she had to get far enough away quickly enough not to get killed by it. She knew she could manage part one. It simply required precision flying and hubris, which were both within her wheelhouse. That second bit, though, might get sacrificed to the plan.

The Gliman banked to her left, away from the lich and the other mages, building up the distance needed for a power dive.

The lich's magic had touched Oleg's mind, and it burned deep. Fire raged through his head, blinding him for long moments before it had passed. He struggled to his knees, shaking his head to clear his vision, his mind grasping for his Will.

His mentor stood a dozen paces away, bravely fending off the lich's assault but losing ground with each passing second.

A lash of acid-green magic slipped through the Curator's defenses and ripped at his left shoulder. The man screamed as arcane flames tore at his clothes and flesh, but miraculously his Will remained focused and his shields stayed in place, sparing him from further damage.

The lich stalked lazily toward its prey, its magic continuing to strike the Curator's shields with abandon.

I have to help. Oleg pushed to his feet. His vision blurred, but not before he had located what he needed.

A large rock a meter long and half as wide rested nearby.

Oleg focused his Will on the projectile, wrapped his magic around the stone, and murmured the words in Dushara that would turn it into a missile.

The wind rose, but the lich didn't notice. It was too focused on completing its assault.

The Curator was down on one knee, hands up to protect himself. It wasn't a total position of weakness. He presented a smaller silhouette to the lich, allowing the ever-shrinking blue disks to cover more of his body.

Despite that, another blast of lightning got past the shields and connected with the old man's ribs. He grunted in pain and the disks paled even more, the original deep indigo now little more than robin's egg blue.

Oleg forced himself to focus. He reached deep within, deeper than he ever had, and summoned more Will than he'd imagined possible before building and shaping it to his purpose. He felt something tear in his mind, shredding along the line of damage put there by the lich, but he put it aside. He'd look into it later—if there was a later. He applied his Will to the stone.

The boulder ripped free of the earth and flew at the lich's back. Its aim was unerring, and its force was more than enough to rip the undead skeleton apart upon contact, no matter how much magic was sustaining its monstrous body.

Oleg closed his eyes, sighed, and crumpled to his knees, having given all he had.

He never saw Malifa's finger twitch, opening a portal at his back to one of the necromantic planes. He never saw the stone fly into it. Likewise, Oleg never saw the second portal open behind him just before his projectile emerged to tear through his spine and shatter his mortal body.

Most of Oleg's blasted, twisted form came to a stop a few feet from the Curator. The man couldn't do anything to help his protégé. He simply screamed in impotent rage and forced more Will into his shields.

He bit down on the pain in his own body, letting his anger flow into the spell. How many times had he cautioned students against relying on raw emotion to power their magicks? It was a short-lived solution, but when one was out of Will, primal emotion could deliver one last effort. He was rewarded by seeing the lich stop in its tracks. It paused, tilting its skull to the side in consternation.

The Curator screamed again and pressed his momentary advantage. The disks transformed into flying ice-blue hammers and struck the lich, draining the energies from its bones while knocking it off its feet and bouncing the skeleton against the ground.

Malifa's lightning had stopped. It could attack or defend but not both. It raised its hands against the onslaught and summoned a shield to protect its prostrate form before its ability to regenerate was stripped away. At that moment, the Curator and the lich knew the contest had ended. The Curator had exhausted his power, and Malifa had barely begun to tap its reserves. The lich chuckled.

"That was impressive," Malifa admitted, taking a few moments to flick away the last of its opponent's conjured weapons. It regained its feet, bony hands moving as if to dust itself off. "I hadn't expected you to be capable of offense by that point. I thought you were done."

"I suppose I was, but I wasn't fighting for myself."

"Ah," the lich added with a click of its teeth. It directed its gleaming eye sockets at the broken figure of the younger mage. "He meant something to you. I am sorry. I would prefer nobody had to die to see my plan come to fruition, but he started it."

The Curator struggled to find the breath to reply. "We will stop you."

The lich shook its skull. "No. You will try, and you will fail."

With that, Malifa tore open another portal, pulled necromantic power through it, and harnessed it to unleash a scourge of flame and lightning against the Curator. The old man's body shook. His throat strained, and his veins pulsed against his flesh as the energies tore him apart from the inside out.

The lich walked up to the smoldering body he had just incinerated. The old man's heart still beat, but his time was limited. He wasn't the priority, though. The younger mage and *gli Anderlibri* piece were.

Malifa bent and grasped the metal box that contained the Codex fragment, then stood over the ravaged form of the young mage with the exceptional grasp of Dushara.

The lich waved a hand's worth of phalanges past the man's face. "Still alive. Remarkable, and so convenient for me." The body floated off the ground, and the lich opened another magical portal.

The Gliman maintained her position a couple of hundred yards above and behind the lich. Her spell had taken precious moments to prepare, but it was the best chance she'd get to destroy the undead bastard. The other mages had bought her the needed time with their lives.

"Make it count," she muttered and utilized a burst of Will to speed unseen and unheard at Malifa's back.

The lich removed the box from the blackened hand of the German mage, then focused its attention on the younger mage's body, causing it to rise off the ground. As she closed the distance between them, the Gliman saw it open another portal into its necromantic realm. Malifa gestured at the portal and drew something into the world from that other plane.

A soul bottle.

"No!" she screamed as she collided with the lich like a dozen linebackers hitting a practice dummy.

The force of the blow knocked the wind out of the Gliman and sent the lich's skeletal body skipping across the earth in one direction as the soul bottle bounced away in another.

She didn't let up. She didn't dare. The Gliman had shoved her hands through Malifa's ribcage on impact and tumbled with him. She hadn't wanted to knock the lich down, but for her spell to work, she had to weave it into the monster's physical being. She pulled its left arm back and grabbed its hand, wrapping both of hers into a clutched fist around the outermost phalanx of what had once been its pinkie.

The lich turned its skull to face the Gliman, the emerald glow within its sockets bright with what she hoped was fear. She shouted the last words of her incantation, drove her remaining Will into the lich's finger bone, and let go. The tiny bone pulsed with a lavender light.

Malifa's skull shifted again, and its glowing eye sockets regarded its hand. "You dare?" Its voice echoed with outrage. Then the lich slapped a hand against the Gliman's chest and sent a burst of magic into her. She flew back, as limp and helpless as a sock in a tornado, only to slam shoulder-first into the Djinn block with a wet thud before crumpling to the ground.

Despite the blow, she did not lose consciousness or take her eyes off of the lich's glowing hand. There was no way to stop it.

The spell would run its course, and she was far too close. So much for part two. The Gliman winced at the thought of the upcoming explosion. It would level the Djinn blocks and likely collapse the ancient city of Petra. Part of her mind wondered if a skilled speaker of Dushara might be able to do something about the resulting radiation that would fill the area.

"Tick-tock, asshole."

The lich shook its skull at her, then it opened another portal and shoved its hand inside. An instant later the portal closed, severing its hand by shearing through the radius and the ulna.

There was no explosion. There was no flash of light and flame. No trumpet of Armageddon. There was only the sound of the desert wind and the labored breathing of dying men. The Gliman lay helpless as Malifa rose to its feet and stalked back to Oleg's prone figure.

She tried to rise but couldn't muster the strength. She'd given everything to the spell, and moreover, the pain in her shoulder threatened to produce unconsciousness at any moment.

"Don't touch him!"

The lich regarded her as it retrieved the soul bottle and placed it on the ground beneath its victim's floating body. The gray fluid in the bottle boiled as it absorbed the essence of the Dushara-speaking mage, then took on a blue-green tint and stilled. That quickly, Malifa had captured the mage's soul.

"I don't expect you to understand. There's no way you could, not limited by a mortal body and mortal sentimentality. I had only the barest glimmering, just enough to transform and attain the needed perspective. I'll dumb it down for you. You deserve to know that much. The possibilities that open up through combining multiple forms of magic at their highest levels will reshape the world. More, they will save it. That's a goal you and I share, I believe. The difference between us is I'm willing to do what it takes. I will end suffering, hunger, and sorrow. I alone will feed the world. I will free us from want."

The Gliman gritted her teeth and pushed herself to a sitting position. "At what cost?"

The lich shrugged, an oddly minimal rising and falling of its collarbone. "Ah, yes. There is always a cost."

Without another word, it snatched the box containing the Dushara piece of the *Demon Codex* and held it in the crook of its damaged arm. With a gesture of its remaining hand, it opened a portal from which a pair of shuffling zombies emerged. Without comment, one guided the comatose body of the young mage through the air, and the other appropriated his bottled soul. Both returned through the portal, following their master back into the realm of the dead.

The light from the portal faded, and the Gliman closed her eyes and succumbed to the pain and frustration of her failure.

CHAPTER TWENTY-ONE

PPP National Park, Iceland
The sun set moments before Watson parked the rented SUV as far from the light posts as possible and turned the engine off. He exited and walked to the rear of the vehicle, where he looked around to make sure he was alone before opening the hatch.

Even with all the seats folded down, Aron still needed every available inch of space. The yeti groaned gratefully as he extricated himself from the vehicle, requiring Watson's assistance to wriggle and unfold his anatomy into the open air. Watching the whole process would give one an appreciation for unpacking twenty clowns from a tiny circus car, but eventually, it was accomplished. Both filed the experience away as a thing neither would speak of again.

The pristine Icelandic air buoyed their spirits, and the pair hiked in companionable silence through the park to the top of the Öxarárfoss waterfall. Watson walked to the edge and stared at the moonlit waters below.

"This place is amazing. This country is so beautiful."

Aron nodded. "Aye, it is—for now."

"What do you mean?"

The yeti swept a massive arm toward the horizon. "Can you not feel it? Your world strains its pieces with an unhurried pace that sings within me."

Watson arched an eyebrow. "I'm sorry?"

"Tectonic plates, Watson. We do not have them in my realm."

"How did your continents form?"

"They did not," explained Aron. "The core of my world is cold. We only have floating islands that emerged from what you would call biomass. Vast plains of buoyant fungi that other life crawled onto out of the oceans and where they learned to breathe the air."

Watson shrugged. "Biology isn't my area of expertise."

Aron cast him a withering side-eye. "You continue to disappoint me, Watson. It is hardly a strong argument for helping you."

"I wouldn't have come to you if I thought there was another way."

"You came for my pages."

"I did, at first. I now see that was a mistake."

The yeti's mouth opened in a terrifying grimace and he laughed. It was a loud bark that in another age would have caused the locals to imagine the noise had curdled the milk and made them certain demons were prowling the countryside. In a very real sense, one was.

"A human admitting to error? The novelty intrigues me. Do go on."

"Don't misunderstand me. I am very concerned that your portion of the *Demon Codex* will ultimately come to the attention of an undead mage, Iosefa Malifa. He's responsible for a lot of recent death and destruction. There's a good chance I've led him to you."

"Why would you do such a thing, Watson?"

"Because I'm a fool."

Aron snorted. "You are flawed and hasty like most humans,

and it is fair to say I judge your species harshly at the best of times, but I do not think you are a fool, even by human standards."

"Malifa and I have known each other for most of our lives. He knows how I think, and he has shown that he knows what course of action I'll take before I figure it out myself. I thought he wouldn't anticipate me coming here to seek your portion of the *Codex*, but I now suspect he planned on it."

"Ah, I now understand. You do not believe you can trust your own judgment."

"Not when it comes to outwitting Malifa, no."

"Is that why you brought me here? Closer to your continent than I have ever been?"

"I need you to come back with me. If I am to have any hope of stopping him, I need your insight. More simply, I need guidance this necromancer cannot anticipate. Your foreign mind and incredible lifespan offer a perspective he can't emulate."

"Hmm," the yeti rumbled. "What of my magic?"

"It can't hurt as long as it doesn't fall into Malifa's hands. That's part of why I sought you out. I don't think he can trap a non-human soul."

Aron slowly nodded his large head. "Yes. That seems right. His energies would not sing to those of life from other realms."

"Also, if it comes down to a fight, I suspect your innate mastery of Hægt would come in handy."

The yeti looked at Watson. "Do you not still speak Hægt as well?"

Watson shrugged. "I do, thanks to you. However, I've studied enough languages and interacted with enough demons to know that native affinity can't be replicated. I don't know if it's the language or a tie to the magic of one's native plane, but it makes a difference."

Aron nodded sagely. "You are correct."

"So, will you help me?"

The yeti swept his gaze across the horizon. "Your world is a beautiful place. I have come to love it, and I will not abandon it to forces as dark as those this lich wishes to impose. I will help you, Derrick Watson. Where do you propose we begin?"

Watson pointed at the horizon. "Near my home. He'll return there since it's his home as well and the location of his earthly assets, or because he wants to taunt me from close range. Either way, he'll show up."

"I suppose that makes sense for a human. Very well, I will travel to your homeland."

"Now for the hard part. I need to figure out how to get you to Philadelphia. I have some ideas—"

The yeti held up a massive hand. "Hush, Derrick Watson. If this Malifa knows you so well, then whether he knows of my existence or not, he will likely assume you will seek help from an outside source. By coming to me, you are still following the paths he envisioned for you. Tell me nothing. Offer no advice. Make no attempt to further guide or influence me. In this way, you conjure a new future for yourself that he cannot foresee."

"That makes sense, but it doesn't change the practical difficulties of getting you to Pennsylvania. Logistics are a bitch and hardly my specialty."

"Having you solve them would be more of you doing what Malifa imagines you might. You would be forced to make use of the resources you have available, which contributes to your predictability. Leave it to me. Go home, Derrick Watson. I will find you and reveal myself when you need me."

Before Watson could object, the yeti sang a low, haunting note that caused time to slow and then stop. Snowflakes hung suspended in the air. Aron patted the human lightly on the head and vaulted over the rail. He advanced to the edge of the overhang, gazed down at the turbulence of the waterfall, and flung himself into the air. At first, he glided as much as fell, but ultimately, even his slow magic was not proof against gravity. He plummeted through the darkness and entered the river beyond the waterfall. As the flow of time reasserted itself, the yeti let the current carry him toward the gap between continents and was gone.

CHAPTER TWENTY-TWO

SCI Greene, Franklin Township, Pennsylvania
The Pennsylvania supermax prison sprawled across the rural countryside north of the border with West Virginia, where it claimed responsibility for almost half the jobs in the former coal country. The bright lights of its perimeter illuminated long stretches of tall fences topped with razor wire. Guard towers stood sentinel over the man-made hell that housed the majority of the state's death row inmates and, thanks to a contract with the feds, its magic-capable inmates as well.

Half a mile down the street from the prison, in the Wal-Mart parking lot, Albert shuddered and stared out his windshield. "No matter how much evidence piles up about how broken their system is, Americans still put people to death. Including more than a few innocent people. I'll never understand it."

H.H. sat on the dashboard, alternately shoving one front paw and then the other into one of the air vents for no apparent reason. "Now you know how long-lived races feel about humans. You're all passion and no judgment. Your species spends so much time and energy on science, but then you turn right around and work even harder to ignore what you learn when it doesn't support what you *want* to hear."

Albert shrugged. "We're stupid. What can I say? But we need to focus."

"Says the guy with raging ADHD."

"Shut up."

H.H. shrugged.

"I have to speak with Jason Holloway. I've run through all the other options, and none of them come close. I *need* his help if I'm going to accelerate my elemental magic."

"And he's in there." H.H. pointed in the direction of the prison. "Behind all those fences and the humorless guards with the guns and so many locked doors you'd think they'd picked them up on sale from this Wal-Mart every morning on their way into work. You know, I think they call it a *super*max prison for a reason. Don't downplay this, Al. You're not fooling me. You could get yourself killed doing this."

He stared at the prison. H.H. was right. Albert didn't deny the risk, but he didn't have an option.

"Then you'd better do your best to help me pull it off."

The imp threw its paws in the air. "Not the reply I was looking for, Al! Seriously, I know some major elemental demons. Not by name, mind you, not so you could summon them, but we could meet up on a neutral plane. I could introduce you. We'll chat. It would be safer than this foolishness."

"We don't have time to debate this, H.H. My mind is made up. It's now or never."

"If I get a vote, let the record show I cast mine for the 'never' option."

"Since when do imps endorse democratic decision-making?"

"We don't. Too messy, but it was worth a shot. Okay then, have you given any thought to an actual plan? Like, what spells do you think you might use? Do you have enough magic to sustain them? Do you have enough Will for everything this is going to require? Have you doubled all those numbers in case some part of this goes horribly wrong?"

Albert sighed. "Well, we know there are two main types of illusion. The first is to alter human perception through their sensory organ, faking what the eyes, ears, etc. perceive. The second and much more difficult is altering the energies those organs detect."

"You'll need the second to fool the cameras. Right?"

"Correct. I can fool humans with the easy stuff, but electronics are another matter."

"You haven't tried this much magic yet. It's reckless and stupid. Did I mention that? It's not a good match like that peanut butter and chocolate thing. Reckless. Stupid."

"This is why humans have aphorisms. Like, 'no pain, no gain,' and 'fortune favors the bold.'"

"You're just emphasizing the stupid part." H.H. jumped off the car's dashboard and landed on its master's shoulder, then dug into the shirt's fabric with all four paws.

Albert screwed a look of determination on his face, and a moment later, he bent light around himself to render them both invisible.

H.H. piped up, "It's gonna look funny when the car door opens and closes itself, don't you think?"

"You aren't helping."

"Yeah, well, you aren't concentrating."

Albert exited the car and strutted invisibly across the parking lot and down the half-mile to the prison's staff parking and the employee entrance to the main facility. He took up position near the door and waited.

It didn't take long for the door to open. A large, slovenly man in a prison guard's uniform exited. The fellow looked like he hadn't slept in days and had been wearing the same uniform for more than twice that long. The guard and his clothes could both do with a good wash. The mage made an effort not to get too close as he slipped past the man and through the door as it was closing.

The next room posed a conundrum. It only had two doors, including the one he had entered through. The other was on the far side of a metal detector, an x-ray machine, and two bored and unhappy uniformed men. Guards. With guns. One sat at a control panel behind bullet-proof glass.

Albert shuffled silently to a corner to watch and figure out his options.

He hadn't leapt into this blind, and H.H. knew it. Albert had watched the prison entrance for the last two days and timed his arrival to coincide with a shift change. The idea—there wasn't enough of it to glorify it by calling it a plan—was to take advantage of the movement and confusion. That was why he wasn't surprised when the far door buzzed, and the man in the booth responded seconds later by opening it.

A pair of guards, joking with the relief of the end of their shift, came through the door and stepped to the exit that led to the parking lot. The far door slowly closed on hydraulic hinges and only then did the outer door open to let the men leave.

"Airlock protocol. That's helpful," H.H. whispered in his ear.

Albert nodded in silent agreement before working his way around the security equipment to position himself closer to the inner door. He held his breath as he crept within arm's reach of the guard. A moment later, he was positioned with his back against the wall less than a yard from the inner door.

Seconds ticked by before Albert heard the door buzz again. It opened and more guards filed through, talking about fantasy football and happy to be heading home, one of them waxing lyrical about a pot roast his wife would be making for dinner that night. The moment they passed, Albert snuck through the open door and into the prison.

It took a while for Albert to work his way across the inner grounds to the Special Housing Unit (SHU), where a very helpful site on the dark web had indicated the prison was keeping Jason. It wasn't a death row unit, but it didn't lack security either. Fortunately, all that security depended on humans doing things correctly. Albert had prepared spells guaranteed to initiate and amplify human error.

"Watch this," he whispered as he stood on the manicured prison lawn outside the SHU that contained Jason. Albert triggered the first illusion he had prepared and thrust a small amount of Will into its casting. A moment later, a man garbed in a straitjacket and nothing else ran down the sidewalk that cut through the middle of the campus.

"Am I supposed to be impressed?" asked H.H.

"Wait for it."

A few seconds ticked by, then all hell broke loose. The front door of every cell block flew open, and uniformed prison guards charged into the night in pursuit of his illusion. The SHU in front of him was no exception. Albert slipped through the open door as a pair of morbidly obese men ran out.

"That should keep them busy."

"It's a start," H.H. muttered.

"Correct. I'm not done."

Before the door could close, Albert unleashed two more illusory jacketed streakers on the campus. The floodlights kicked on, and Albert took advantage of the added illumination to magically scoop up pieces of shadow and send them careening among the guards. Confused, angry shouting drifted to his ears before the large metal door of the SHU swung shut.

Once inside, Albert had to dodge as another guard came to the door to peer through its reinforced window and watch the chaos unfolding in the expansive courtyard. He compared the scene to a monitor on the wall displaying the same view and frowned. The mage stepped away quietly and surveyed the interior of the SHU.

It wasn't complicated. In addition to the electronically sealed exit to the outside, there was one more door. It was similarly secured and controlled by an officer who sat within an adjacent booth, little more than a protected bubble with an array of video monitors. Beyond that enclosure, a single huge room housed the prisoners.

Albert counted sixty-four cells divided evenly between two tiers, upper and lower. The cells were little more than black metal boxes, each with a white metal door that contained a square of reinforced glass that let guards peer inside and see the entirety of the shallow rooms. Metal catwalks and stairs and a few walls connected the two levels of boxes. Every cell had a number painted on its door in black numerals twelve inches tall.

He looked at the upper tier and confirmed what the website had told him. The higher you went, the higher the numbers of the associated cells. The surrounding catwalk was five feet wide and bordered by steel guardrails. His eyes tracked from door to door.

Cell Fifty-two. There it was.

H.H. whispered into Albert's ear, "How do you plan to get in there?"

"They have to do rounds at some point," he whispered back in frustration.

The guard peering out the door swung his head in Albert's direction. He stared at the wall where the mage stood, cloaked in invisibility.

Albert held his breath. The man finally returned his attention to the show unfolding in the courtyard.

That had been close.

A few minutes went by, then the guard in the booth leaned over, and his metallic voice came through the speakers. "Mac, we gotta do rounds."

The guard at the door shrugged and reluctantly straightened. "All right. Tell me what's happening."

"Ha! Will do. Right now, it looks like they're chasing ghosts."

"What do you mean? They're chasing a bunch of naked guys. They must have gotten out of the psych ward. Jones is working over there tonight, and I'll bet you a week's pay that this is his mess. That jerk could fuck up a wet dream."

"I can't see them on the camera. How many guys were there?"

"At least three, but ask me if I'm shocked that our multimillion-dollar cameras aren't functioning. State of the art, my ass!"

"You got that right."

Mac shrugged and walked to the inside door as the buzzer sounded. He hauled it open and entered the interior of the SHU, with Albert close on his heels. Once inside, Albert allowed Mac to get well ahead of him.

"I'm going to let him go past Jason's cell," he whispered.

"How long can you keep this up?"

"I don't know."

"That's comforting. You know they design prisons to keep people in, right? Maybe you should drop the illusions and save your energy."

"Good call." With a thought, Albert dismissed the illusions by having them run into the shadows behind buildings before disappearing. Next, he withdrew the extra shadows he'd created, which made it easier for the guards to waste time searching for straitjacketed runners who weren't there.

"That should keep them busy for a bit."

"Let's hope you have that long. Now go. The guard's about to pass Jason's cell."

Albert hustled over to Cell Fifty-two. He peered inside and saw Jason, one of Professor Watson's past doctoral students, reclining on a metal bunk that was welded to the wall. He had a book with a small reading lamp clipped to it. The buzzer sounded back at the entrance, and Albert glanced over his shoulder and down a level to see Mac returning to the building's foyer, his rounds complete.

Albert concentrated and used his Will to push an image of himself into Jason's mind. Then he rapped gently on the pane of shatterproof glass set into the door. The mage sat up with a look of alarm on his face. He hastily set his book down and approached the door, where he leaned his ear close to the frame and whispered, "Albert? What the hell are you doing?"

"Don't worry. They can't see me. To them, I'm invisible. It's an illusion. You think you see me, but that's a different illusion."

"What? How?"

"Jason, I'm sorry, but I don't have much time. Just trust me. I've learned a lot of new tricks lately. I...*we* need your help."

"I doubt it." Jason sighed. "The last time I tried to help, a bunch of innocent people died. Also, in case you haven't noticed, I'm in prison. They don't exactly encourage initiative here, let alone community service."

Albert shrugged at the irony. "You can't undo the past, Jason, but you can atone, and maybe keep more people from dying."

"What are you talking about?"

"Professor Watson believes that Malifa—well, technically, the lich that used to be Malifa—is still out there, tracking down the rest of *gli Anderlibri*, and it's only a matter of time before he uses them to cause even more trouble."

"You think I can do something to help? Or you can?"

Albert paused. He wasn't ready for anyone to know his plan, but he had to tell Jason something. "Not me, but I know another mage who can. He sent me to ask you for a spell structure that only a fluent speaker of Mem could craft."

"That's exactly the magic I used when I got those people killed, Albert. No way."

"Jason, please! Malifa is *guaranteed* to kill more people. He doesn't care how many. He's batshit-crazy, you know? We have to stop him, and we can't do it without a fight. He already holds more weapons than we do. If we're to have any chance of evening the odds, we need you to help us."

Jason paced his cell in agitation. Albert wiped the sweat from his forehead, and the movement wasn't lost on his familiar.

"You're getting tired, Al. You need to hurry this up," H.H. hissed into his ear.

"I know. I'm fine. I can do this."

Jason didn't know about the effort Albert was expending and wasn't in any hurry. He continued to pace, rubbing the shaggy beard that had grown to cover his cheeks and chin since Albert had last seen him.

Albert's left hand fluttered reflexively. He grasped it with his right hand to hold it still before the imp noticed and berated him again. He didn't need the added distraction.

Jason finally returned to the window. "What do you want to know?"

With relief, Albert explained his needs.

"I can do that," acknowledged Jason. He whispered instructions through the cell door and had just finished when the buzzer sounded, signaling that rounds were beginning again.

"Albert, you need to get out of here. That's all the help I can give you. I hope it's enough."

"It'll have to be," Albert whispered as he placed an illusory palm on the glass. Jason held his hand against Albert's. "Take care of yourself, Jason."

With that, he headed for the exit, desperately hoping Mac wouldn't take too long on his rounds.

CHAPTER TWENTY-THREE

Alexander University, Philadelphia

Watson looked at himself in the antiquated mirror in his office bathroom and sighed. "You look like hell. I bet you haven't slept in days. It's probably not a good sign that you're talking to yourself either."

He splashed water on his face and ran a damp comb through his hair in a desperate attempt to feel more human. He returned to his office, where he continued speaking aloud like he was leading a graduate seminar and hoping to inspire his students with his take on the Socratic method.

"There has to be a way to outsmart him. Something he can't predict. Maybe if I'd managed to sleep more on the flight back, I'd have come up with something. I just need to let my mind relax for a little bit. Yeah…"

The professor collapsed on his couch and had just managed to pull a blanket over himself when Trixie let herself in without knocking.

"So much for that idea," he mumbled.

"Say what?"

"Nothing. I'm just happy to see you."

Trixie arched an eyebrow at him before she plopped on the floor alongside the couch. "Honey, you look awful."

"That sounds accurate. Painful to hear, but accurate."

"Why didn't you call me from the airport? I'd have come to get you."

"I didn't want to be a bother. I'd hoped to unwind on the cab ride here."

"Did you?"

He replied with a sheepish shrug.

"Have you gotten any sleep?"

"Not really. The fate of the world keeps getting in the way."

She smiled, and seeing her expression did more for him than a brief nap would have. Then the smile faded, and she came at him again. She was the more rational of the two just then.

"Derrick, you won't be any good to anyone if you don't take care of yourself. How can you save the world if you can't even function?"

Watson grunted noncommittally.

Trixie held up her hands and sighed. "Okay. I didn't come here to harass you."

"That's a relief."

"Don't get snarky just because you're tired and grumpy. I came here to apologize."

"For what? You didn't do anything wrong."

"For the way I acted when you proposed. Don't misunderstand me. It was a stupid thing for you to do. Stupid. I wasn't expecting that, and you know how little I like surprises. That one? That was a really big one."

Watson sat up and dropped the blanket. The nap wasn't going to happen; that much was certain. "Okay, Trixie. I appreciate what you're saying, even the *stupid* part, and I understand, but my brain is kinda fried right now, and I can't figure out where this leaves us."

The young woman took his hands. "It leaves us where we left

off. I love you. You love me. Until we work out all this stuff with Malifa, that needs to be enough."

Watson stood at the mention of the necromancer, pulling Trixie up with him. He released her hands and paced around his office.

"Yeah, you're right. It all comes back to Malifa. I have to figure this out."

Trixie took a deep breath. "Well, maybe I could help if you'd tell me what's going on. I don't know what you've been up to or why it all means you can't sleep. Fill me in. Please."

"I went to talk to some people." He kept pacing as he explained. "People I thought could help us and add to what we might accomplish with Dani and Stanley and Albert. After I struck out with the first one, Malifa appeared."

"Appeared? Where?"

"In my hotel room in Beijing. He'd somehow tracked me."

"What did he want?"

Watson grunted. "To taunt me. To make himself feel superior. To show how smart he is."

"What an ass."

"Yeah, but he wasn't wrong. He's been one step ahead of me the whole time. That's why I went to Iceland next, to get some outside perspective."

"Did it help?"

"Not yet."

"What does that mean?"

"It means I got an offer of help. I don't know what it's going to look like or where it will appear."

"Derrick, that doesn't sound very helpful."

"I know, but that's exactly why it might end up being the most helpful thing of all. If I can't second guess it, maybe Malifa can't either."

"Well, what do we do next?"

"I have to find a way to stop him."

Trixie stepped in front of him, forcing him to choose between halting or running her down. He stopped. She crossed her arms. "You do know it's annoying that you keep saying 'I' and 'me' instead of 'we' and 'us,' right?"

"I'm not trying to be exclusionary or insulting. It's just, nobody knows him like I do. Nobody understands him the way I do. That's why it's up to me to stop him."

"What about the mage cops? What about other mages who have more experience with this sort of thing? Why does it have to be Derrick-freaking-Watson against the biggest Evil of the Century? Why isn't it someone else's responsibility?"

"Because they'll all fail. I just told you, I'm the only one with the necessary knowledge to stop him."

"Honey, I know you believe that. Maybe it's even true, but it hasn't done much good yet, has it?"

Watson sighed. Hard as it was to admit, she was right. He reminded himself that she usually was.

CHAPTER TWENTY-FOUR

The Haven, Tuscany

The Librarian sat at the desk in the personal book room that contained some of Dee's surviving original volumes and the generations of commentary that had been written about them. It was the heart and soul of magical research, and she used it as her working office. She chewed the tip of the earpiece of her glasses and regarded the three mages standing opposite her. She was separated from them by the marble-topped expanse of antique desk and generations of secrets compiled by hundreds of practitioners. These three were the latest to bring her interesting news of the Gliman, and she considered their reports very carefully.

The trio of mages, all advisors and operatives in the Folio, waited patiently. Finally, the Librarian turned to Kesi, a tall, lithe, dark-skinned mage from Kenya. "You're telling me she's *not* a terrorist?"

"No, ma'am. Not exactly. As best we can determine, those claims emerged as part of a disinformation/smear campaign by the individuals and institutions she opposed, blocked, or outed for greed, corruption, and/or incompetence. At a minimum, the allegations of deaths were either wholly fabricated or gravely exaggerated. Pardon the pun."

The Librarian waved it away. "But she *can* create fissionable materials?"

"Oh, yes. All our sources agree on that."

"Bombs?"

"There is no doubt. It's like she's made a point of allowing outside agencies to confirm that."

"Why? What possible advantage could she derive from letting her enemies know she has that capability?"

The operatives exchanged glances. Finally, a young man who looked like he had come from a Viking documentary cleared his throat to explain.

"Our best guess, ma'am, is that she put the information out there as a deterrent."

"That doesn't make her a terrorist, Detmer? Explain."

"We think it was modeled on an earlier Cold War stance: letting her opposition know what she is capable of without having to resort to a nuclear response. Essentially, it's just saber-rattling."

"You're saying she has a 'no first strike' policy. That she's been bluffing all this time?"

"Not about her capability, just in respect to using it. As far as we can determine—and the three of us are in agreement on this point and arrived at our assessments independently—she's never killed anyone."

"Oh, please. How is that possible?"

Detmer shrugged, then glanced at the other two operatives. "We believe it's part of her façade. She's battered quite a few people, roughed some up, perhaps broke a few limbs, but even there, she hasn't played favorites. Her actions have been directed across the full political spectrum. She doesn't seem to have an ideology other than to punish those who use power in a corrupt and abusive fashion. Frankly, from most perspectives, her targets deserved what they got."

The Librarian nodded. Past pieces fell into place, promising more would follow. "She has always acted in pursuit of an objectively higher cause or the greater good?"

"Yes, ma'am. We found no evidence to the contrary."

"Always as a lone wolf, so to speak?"

"Yes, ma'am. That is accurate."

The Librarian leaned forward, removed her glasses, and placed them on the desk as she rubbed the bridge of her nose, a ritual she associated with an imminent migraine. "This situation is intolerable."

"Ma'am?"

"It won't do. The Gliman has repeatedly demonstrated that she cannot be contained. Left to her own devices, she's a dangerous wildcard and a liability. She'll either have to evolve or be ended. If she won't serve us, I cannot risk her becoming a tool of the Scorpion."

CHAPTER TWENTY-FIVE

New York City, New York

Albert left his train at Penn Station. He walked briskly through the entrance hall with its grand columns and marble floor to the taxi line, then climbed into the back of a cab. A short time later, he and H.H. were deposited on 5th Avenue outside the Metropolitan Museum of Art. He paid the fare in cash and included a generous tip, but not so generous as to stand out in the driver's memory.

As he shivered in the autumn breeze, the mage tried to focus on the task ahead. Now that he stood on the edge of the moment, his familiar's nagging doubts surfaced in his thoughts.

"I hope this works, my friend."

"That's one of us."

Albert balked. "What? You *want* me to fail?"

"Of course not. Failure would be bad in lots of ways that could mess you up mentally and emotionally and magically and physically. I'm hoping for a middle ground between failure and success."

"You want me to play it safe. That's what I've *been* doing."

"I know, but if this works, you're going to become the lich's *numero uno* target, Al. I've been to multiple planes of existence, and I have never met anyone who would envy that position."

"Well, do you have a better idea?"

"Yeah! Go back to Philly and order a pizza or find that food truck that makes those amazing grilled cheese sandwiches. Even a salad would be better than this."

Albert shook his head. "You just don't get it. This isn't an accident. Malifa. My magic coming into bloom. It's no coincidence. I'm destined to play a role in this."

"Look, I'm not saying there's no such thing as destiny, but it's not something you can count on, and it sure isn't anything you plan on. Destiny is a word you only use in hindsight."

"No, destiny is accepting you have a role to play in the larger scheme of things."

"Well, I hope it's a role with a happy ending and pretty women because the role of a zombie sucks. If you lose to a necromancer, that's probably the best outcome you can hope for."

Albert didn't reply. There wasn't anything to say. Dire and pessimistic as it was, his familiar wasn't wrong. That didn't mean it was right, either.

He entered the Met and ignored the signage promoting the latest exhibits, instead seeking a much more mundane destination: the men's bathroom. He let himself in and waited for the facility's only other occupant to depart before he entered a stall and flipped the latch on the door. "Bar the exit. Don't let anyone inside."

"I know the plan." The imp huffed. "Just get on with it. We need to complete this foolishness and leave ASAP. Don't forget *that* part of the plan. Time matters. The clock's ticking, Al."

The young mage nodded and closed his eyes. In the interest of brevity and escaping before Malifa showed up, he had prepared the sequence of illusions in advance. All that remained was for him to summon his Will and pair it with a triggering incantation.

A few seconds ticked by as H.H. nervously paced atop the

toilet paper dispenser. Its focus wasn't within the stall, though. It was magically locking the outer door three different ways. No one would get in on its watch, no matter how desperately they needed to pee!

A muffled boom rocked the stall as magic radiated from the bathroom. Albert's illusion manifested on the steps outside the museum.

An image of Asombro strutted out of the entrance and toward the fountain on 5th Avenue. His right hand was raised to the sky, and gouts of fire erupted from his fingertips. The flames darted forward to interweave with the water of the fountain in a dance that was eerie and breathtaking. Even so, half the tourists ran away in terror. The locals just shrugged. Life in New York.

In his left hand, Asombro clutched pages of the *Demon Codex*.

"Iosefa Malifa! Hear me! I am Asombro! I know your power is great and that you listen with the ears of those who have passed. My words will reach you in time. I have some skills myself, a mastery of all five elemental realms, a range not seen in centuries. I offer them to you in service to your greater vision. I know you seek to meld different realms of magic to achieve possibilities not dreamt of since the time of John Dee. Let me share what I've learned about merging the elements into a single whole. Seek me out and let me join your cause."

A wind whipped up from nowhere and struck the remaining bystanders, pushing them away from the mage. The wind swirled around Asombro next and flung him into the air. He disappeared from view and also from existence. The flames he'd conjured vanished. The fountain resumed its normal display.

In the stall, Albert groaned and opened his eyes. "How are we doing for time?"

H.H. consulted a miniature pocket watch it withdrew from a cheek pouch. "If we leave now, we should be fine. Are you okay?"

"Just tired. I should be able to sleep on the plane. Go ahead and unlock the door. I'll be along in a moment."

Albert's appearance shimmered. A frail man who was decades older emerged from the bathroom stall and departed the Met with a hamster concealed in the pocket of his nondescript coat. He hailed a cab and headed to the airport. When he exited, he held a suitcase that hadn't been there when he'd gotten in and wouldn't exist after he'd checked it. The ticket he presented at the counter claimed he was John Velcado. His passport matched the new name and his appearance. He boarded the plane and settled into his seat, patting the pocket that contained three first-class tickets to other countries, each in a different name. Asombro would visit them over the next couple of days, thus baiting the trap. That was the plan.

CHAPTER TWENTY-SIX

Butcher and Singer Restaurant, Philadelphia

The restaurant was immaculate and posh. Watson's dining companions fit right in. Trixie was beautiful in a simple sleeveless black A-line dress, while Dani and Stanley rocked a pair of stylish suits. Watson ordered a dozen oysters for the table and watched the waitress depart with their drink order before sweeping the others with his gaze, signaling the end of casual conversation. "This isn't purely a social call. I asked you to join me tonight for a serious reason."

"Malifa." Trixie's tone made it unclear if the name was a statement or a question.

Watson grunted in acknowledgment. "Malifa. As you all know, he's dead but not done."

Dani and Stanley shivered and reached for the other's hand under the table, gripping tightly.

"I thought he was done with us," said Dani. "He got what he wanted, didn't he? He's immortal now."

Watson shook his head. "Becoming a lich was the first step of a larger plan. Iosefa has never lacked for ambition, even in undeath, it seems. He wants to control all the magic that leaks into our world from the other realms."

"That makes no sense." Stanley frowned. "He's a necromancer. He doesn't have the language ability to control the other kinds of magic."

"That didn't stop him from using you both." Trixie winced as she said it.

"That's the thing. It doesn't matter if he can achieve control. He's moving forward as if he can—if not now, then at some point in the future. It's a vast and twisted game to him. He's marshaling his forces in preparation and expanding his options."

Stanley frowned. "Meaning what?"

"Based on what he told me, he's removing pieces from the board. I believe he plans to start actively killing mages so that when he finds other fragments of the *Demon Codex*, regardless of which ones, he'll have a clearer path to using them."

Dani pulled her hand free from Stanley's and brought both of hers onto the table to grasp Watson's. "Professor, are you in danger? Is there anything we can do to help? You know him better than anyone. What do you advise?"

Watson sighed and deflated as the waitress returned with their drinks. He remained silent while glasses were placed on the table, waiting for the server to move on. "That's the problem. I might know Malifa, but he knows me too, and as I'm discovering, better than I know myself. That is why I don't think he's targeting me. Despite trading away most of his humanity, enough of who he used to be remains that he derives significant satisfaction from taunting me. He goes out of his way to reveal that he's always ahead of anything I come up with. Call it a character flaw. He did it at the nut warehouse and again at the water treatment plant, and he's still doing it despite being a lich."

"What about Albert?" asked Dani. "Shouldn't he be here too?"

"That would have been my preference, but he's taken time off. I only found out this morning via voice mail."

"Time off for what?"

Watson shrugged. "Traveling. That's about all he told me. He's had a hard time since making changes to his medications, and I've been giving him space."

"That makes sense," agreed Dani. "He and I talked about it, and with H.H.'s help, I've been monitoring him. He'll be fine."

The others nodded as they considered that news. Then Stanley asked, "Where does that leave us?"

"As independents," explained Watson. "You can't rely on what I say because I have to assume Malifa will already have figured out any strategies I might come up with. If I know that he's operating several moves ahead of me, then the best thing is for me not to engage with him, not to play the game at all."

Trixie frowned. "How are you supposed to fight him if you don't do anything? I mean, I get what you're saying, but if the only reason he hasn't killed you is that he wants to toy with you, aren't you throwing away the very thing that's keeping you safe?"

"But that's just it. The best I can hope to do is draw him into a situation where others can take him on."

"Which is what you mean by all of us acting independently." Dani bit her lip, pondering.

Stanley nodded, sipped his drink, and sighed. "There's just one problem with that."

"Oh?"

"What if Malifa foresaw you doing this? What if he knows your next move is not to make any more moves but instead to leave your pieces free and autonomous on the board?"

Watson nodded. "That's a very real possibility, but even if it's true, it doesn't mean he knows what the rest of you will do. No more than I do."

"You think he'll show up even though he knows he's walking into an ambush?"

"I do. He has to. His arrogance guarantees it."

"The problem," noted Trixie, "is that it might not be arrogance."

"What do you mean?"

"He kicked our asses already. It's not arrogance if it's true."

CHAPTER TWENTY-SEVEN

The Haven, Tuscany

The Gliman rested her injured shoulder against the back of an ancient wooden chair next to an open window. A cool evening breeze drifted in from the Ligurian Sea, visible in the sunset beyond the window's frame. The smell of salt air wafted in on a warm breeze, keeping the scents of death and disinfectant at bay.

The estate—she'd learned its name translated from the Italian as "The Haven"—was postcard-perfect, nestled on a hill over the sea an hour west of Florence. If she hadn't been recovering from Malifa handing her ass to her, she would have really enjoyed the ambience. Instead, she was in constant pain and discomfort, though that paled compared to what the man in the bed across the room had suffered in his final hours.

The Librarian, who had introduced herself by that title and no name when the Gliman had awakened, stepped forward and reverently closed the Curator's eyes. Despite a valiant struggle to survive the necromantic wounds inflicted by Malifa, he had succumbed and breathed his last. At least he finally looked at peace.

"A page turns, a chapter ends, but the book endures." The

Librarian whispered the words to the dead man in the bed. After a moment's silence, she turned to the Gliman. "The Folio has lost its Curator."

"I'm sorry for your loss."

The Librarian shook her head. "My loss is for my friend of the past three decades. Our shared loss, though you did not know it, is the skill and integrity he brought to the role. He kept the balance of magic in the world and separated fools from dangerous tools that could blow everything up."

The Gliman arched a brow. "Like me creating fissionable materials?"

"Oh, no, my dear. Not at all, else our departed Curator would have visited you long since. You might be many things and *accused* of being many more but declaring you a fool has never been on anyone's lips. Quite the opposite, which is why I brought you here instead of having you dropped off at a hospital in Jordan. I wanted you to witness the passing of my old friend."

"I don't understand."

"The Curator is dead. The Folio needs a new one. While we usually recruit from within our ranks, I am offering the position to you. If you think you're up to a walk, I'd like to show you some things you should consider as I explain."

Unsurprisingly, the Librarian led the Gliman to an ornate library. One wall, easily twenty feet high, was covered with books. *Ancient* books. Rare books. Books that pulsed with the power of the knowledge they contained. Books that begged to be read, studied, and understood.

On the opposite side of the room, a different aesthetic played out. That wall bore a massive digital display showing a map of the world. Dots glowed in every color. The Librarian waved a hand nonchalantly.

"Here you stand, in the heart of the Order known as the Followers of Saint Andrew, the largest and most public of the so-called secret societies of practitioners in the world. What few outside the Order know is that the leadership of the Folio also operates out of these facilities, and in turn, we share our resources with them. Behind you are tomes of magical history, grimoires, and other texts that speak to the heart of magic in our world. These books contain knowledge long lost to mankind, and in most cases, to the magical world as well. They are the least dangerous volumes in our collections."

The Gliman raised an eyebrow but didn't interrupt. The Librarian turned to the map.

"This shows the combined operational and intelligence picture. Some dots represent our operatives, each one a mage sworn to promote the agenda and goals of the Order."

"What about the other dots?"

"They represent the locations of mages that are, shall we say, practitioners of interest to the Order."

The Gliman snorted at the description. She noted a cluster of blue, green, and red dots near Philadelphia. *Well, that's interesting. I wonder which colors belong to which mages? What color am I?*

"Does that mean your group is part of the Order?"

"Yes and no," replied the Librarian. "For most of its history, the Folio has maintained its numbers by drawing new members from the most accomplished among the Followers of Saint Andrew, a tradition that goes back to the monks who scattered the *Codex* created by John Dee. We serve a higher purpose. We prepare for a specific threat that is beyond the scope of anything those monks could have imagined."

"I'm not part of any group. Why would you offer me a slot? You've surely done your homework and know I don't play well with others."

The Librarian showed no amusement at the remark. She ignored the question and continued her brief. "Dozens of other locations belong to us, independent of St. Andrew's Followers. We have logistics hubs, safe houses, research centers, and secret vaults to secure the most dangerous items in our collections."

"Like the *Demon Codex*," the Gliman interjected.

"Among others, yes, but those are *not* represented on this map. In fact, only three people know the locations where *gli Anderlibri* are secreted. One of them just passed away in the room down the hall."

The Gliman nodded. "How long have you been doing this?"

The Librarian placed her hand on her throat. "Goodness! I've been a member of the Order for over forty years and part of the Folio for the last twenty-seven. I can scarcely remember a time when I wasn't doing this."

"Excuse me. That's incredible, but I didn't mean you personally. I meant the Order. When was it founded?"

"Ah. Well, that goes back a bit further. Frankly, the short answer is we don't know. Our records of the Order's earliest days are incomplete. They were destroyed in wars and by inquisitors and other ignorants in power across the centuries. Others were stolen by governments and likely remain locked away. After the upheavals of the last few decades, they might not realize what they have in their archives.

"We suspect other pieces are squirreled away in private collections. Moreover, for the past few centuries, there has been reason to suspect the various secret societies repeatedly subsumed one another, taking each other's names and members, deliberately and not. One of the more recent iterations of the Order was founded in a town you're familiar with. Philadelphia?"

"Philly? Really?"

The Librarian shrugged. "It began in a tavern, no less. What's the old adage about humble beginnings?"

"You mean a bar? This keeps getting better."

The Librarian allowed herself a small smile. "As I said, this is the current iteration. The Order has been forced to break up and reassemble on multiple occasions. The form you see now was created due to a schism that occurred during your American Revolution."

"Okay, but where did it all begin?"

The Librarian walked to the map and placed a finger on a speck of land in eastern Italy near the Adriatic Sea. "The story starts not far from where we now stand, in San Marino."

"I've heard the name, but I confess it means little to me."

The older woman shrugged delicately. "That isn't surprising. Most people outside the region are unfamiliar with it, but the Republic of San Marino has a rich history, much of it shrouded in secrecy."

"Like the origins of the *Demon Codex*?"

"Correct. Now, if you'd like to take a seat, I'll call for wine and olives while I tell you the story."

"Would you add some Advil to that list, please? My arm is throbbing."

"Of course, dear. My apologies. I should have inquired about your needs sooner."

CHAPTER TWENTY-EIGHT

Washington, DC
Bits of video captured on cellphones outside the Met had spread across the internet and cable news like wildfire. Commentators and pundits generated questions and ratings points for their networks by speculating on what it meant. While everyone knew magic existed, its practitioners were relatively few and rarely demonstrative. Asombro had been extravagant and flamboyant, and his subsequent appearances around the world had kept him at the forefront of speculation. The sun had just set when the now internationally infamous image of Asombro materialized on the top step of the Lincoln Memorial, standing straight and tall, oozing confidence and charisma. Nearby, Albert huddled in a corner, wrapped in the early evening's darkness. H.H. monitored him from its perch on the grad student's shoulder.

Both mage and imp were exhausted. Their travels and massive expenditures of magic had taken their toll, and both were focused on this final appearance of Asombro to complete their overlong tour. They were, understandably, distracted, which went a long way toward explaining their surprise when a massive hairy hand swooped in and snatched the hamster off Albert's shoulder. The fingers of that hand became a loose fist, caging the creature. It moved too fast for the familiar or its mage to prevent the capture, or maybe everything else moved too slowly.

"You are an imp! Why do you smell of Watson? You both do." Another gigantic hand pressed into Albert's chest and pinned him to the wall.

Albert tried to cry out, then tried to push free. He failed at both. The weight holding him in place was too great, and the sudden pressure had crushed the air out of him. He brought his eyes up and flinched as he took in the creature who was half again his height and three times his mass.

In the instant of the attack and question, Albert's Will fell away, and his spells collapsed. Atop the steps of the memorial, Asombro winked out of existence. Albert fought to shift his focus, aided by the burst of fear-fueled adrenaline coursing through him. Flames rippled down his arms, threatening to set the monster on fire.

The hand on his chest pulled back, but it wasn't to let him go. It slammed him back again. "Do not waste your illusions on me. I know the fire is not real."

"Don't be so sure," replied Albert. He rasped the trigger to one of the hanging spells in 'ry that he kept ready, swapping the illusion for the real thing. He backed against the wall as the heat of the fire engulfed the creature.

Time slowed again and Albert fell, shoved aside by the brute as it dropped to the ground. The creature rolled to extinguish the flames, slapping its gigantic hands over its body. Released, the hamster tumbled across the ground, got its feet under it, and raced to the mage's side.

"Albert, stop! It's a demon!"

He staggered to his feet. "Seriously? A demon?"

"Trust me on this. It's the real deal."

"Impossible. Why should that make me feel better? It's not contained. There's no sigil. What's keeping it in our world?"

"Choice," snarled the demon, rising and patting out the last flames. "And debt. I now regret the former and suspect the latter will be paid before the day is out if this is any indication. You are Watson's pup, are you not?"

"I...what, wait! You're the yeti?"

"I am. Call me Aron. I am here to help Derrick Watson. I suppose that includes saving you from yourself."

"Saving me?"

The yeti sighed and gestured at the memorial where Asombro had briefly materialized. "Apparently. What were you thinking with this display?"

"I was trying to draw out the lich."

"Then what?"

"I..."

"We had a plan," insisted H.H., its deep voice echoing off the walls.

"Your plan was based on equal parts stupidity and things Watson knows. Your adversary already possesses Watson's knowledge and can second guess his every intention. The stupidity is the seed of your demise."

"And you have a better plan?" asked H.H. "The kid and I knew Watson left to find a yeti, so if you're right, Malifa knows that too."

"No doubt he does," replied the yeti. "But he cannot know that I came seeking you, and he cannot imagine what we can accomplish together."

"You have a better plan?" Albert repeated.

"I do. I've had several years in the last few days to consider it from every angle. If you are Watson's latest student, I presume you have both talent and sense. Make use of them and listen to what I say. Can you manage that?"

Albert nodded, and H.H. didn't so much as squeak.

"Fine. Here is what we are going to do…"

Trixie sat on the sofa in her dorm's common room, watching television while texting with Dani.

Have you seen this guy on the news?

The one that looks like the cover of a romance novel and is going around declaring his love for Fat Mage all over the globe?

That's the one. Is he crazy? Who is he?

I don't know. Stanley has asked some of his friends at the Bureau if they know anything about him. So far, nada. He's a mystery.

Could he screw up our plans?

I doubt it. But I don't know what to think anymore. The world has clearly gone crazy.

Amen. TTYL.

Trixie picked up the remote and shut off the tv. She shook her head and tried to concentrate. Her homework didn't care if she had to save the world, and even if she thought her alchemy professor might cut her some slack, she didn't want to risk it coming back to bite Derrick in the ass. From what he'd said about the dean that was exactly the sort of ammunition he'd use —a case of not if but when.

Derrick hadn't shown that he was that good at navigating

faculty politics. He might be the smartest man she'd ever met, but he was clueless about some things, as he'd so aptly demonstrated with his recent proposal.

Besides, she didn't want to rely on favors from *anyone* for her coursework. Sighing, she cracked her textbook on the analytical chemistry of transmutation and began reading Chapter Five for the third time.

CHAPTER TWENTY-NINE

The Haven, Tuscany

The effective but contraindicated combination of wine and pain killers did their job. The Gliman felt better and was able to listen intently as the Librarian laid out the back story of the Order of Saint Andrew and *gli Anderlibri.*

She slid her wine glass aside and focused absently on the tray of olives beside it as the older woman started the tale.

"Please understand that what I am about to relay to you is the best information we have. That doesn't mean it is correct."

The Gliman shrugged and broke the skin of an olive with her teeth. "I can handle ambiguity." She spoke around the salty flesh of her snack.

"Good. There will be plenty. I will start at the beginning, in Constantinople."

"Istanbul?"

"The same. Most modern practitioners mistakenly believe the systematic study of magic began with John Dee in the sixteenth century, but that just reflects Western imperialism. It's both easy and unforgivable to ignore or discount the science and exploration that took place in the Middle East while Europe was sliding into the Dark Ages. In the early fifth century, a monk whose identity has been lost to us began to compile a comprehensive list of demonic names. *True* names, complete with lineage. Names of immense power. Thanks to the reach of the empire at the time, he had access to tomes of knowledge that have not survived."

The Gliman leaned back in her chair and sipped her wine. *This is going to be good.*

"As I said, we don't know his name, but we do know that his calling made him an outcast. He fled across the Mediterranean and eventually arrived at the monastic community on Monte Titano that had been founded by Marinus. There, his quest for knowledge was embraced. Note that Marinus was an outcast himself and a stonemason."

"Really. That's interesting in a conspiratorial way. Somebody alert Dan Brown!"

The Librarian snorted. "It is. Our monk continued his work in relative secrecy for years and died in the middle of the century. His work was furthered, though perhaps with less enthusiasm, by other monks over the next thirteen hundred years. The monastery became the center for magical study in the western world.

"Scholars and mages and many others made pilgrimages to Monte Titano. There they learned and mastered demonic languages not taught elsewhere in the world. After they did so, they carried their hard-won knowledge away. At that time, practitioners were rare, few, and solitary, except in this one place."

"Wait. If all of this began in the fifth century, why does everyone credit John Dee as the great forerunner of modern magical inquiry?"

"Because it's known that Dee was among the many pilgrims to the monastery. He visited and contributed to the work and made copies of several manuscripts. He also shared techniques he'd discovered for the preservation of books. Most experts agree that this last bit led to the mistaken notion that the *Demon Codex* was Dee's work, but in fact, it represents the continuous efforts of hundreds of monks from well before Dee's birth to after his death."

"That's a lot of study."

"As you know, it is a difficult and often dangerous field of research."

The Gliman laughed. "True."

"In the seventeenth century, things got difficult."

"More difficult than being cast out of Constantinople during the Dark Ages? What happened?"

"The Church recognized San Marino as an independent republic."

"Just to be clear, you mean Rome, right?"

"Yes. Pope Urban VIII, to be precise."

"Why did San Marino becoming an independent country cause problems for the monks?"

"Because the Church demanded it."

"Oh. That would do it, especially in those days."

"Quite. As a condition of the Vatican's recognition of San Marino's independence, they secured an agreement that not only would magical research come to an end, but the *Demon Codex* would be turned over to Vatican authorities."

"Clearly, that didn't happen," asserted the Gliman.

"No, it did not. We don't know how or by whom, but a decision was made. The monastery could no longer protect the Codex, so they opted to break it into pieces. We can only assume their reasoning was that the possibility of failure meant that surrendering a few individual components would be less dangerous than the capture of the whole volume.

"One or more of the monks smuggled these portions out of San Marino. Thus were born the *Books of Andrew*, or as they were known in the local language, *gli Anderlibri*. Another hundred years passed. Finally, an ill-fated invasion by Cardinal Alberoni forced the Church to admit the *Codex* was no longer within the tiny republic. Since then, members of the Followers of Saint Andrew have worked to keep its knowledge and power out of the hands of those who would abuse it."

"Isn't that pretty much everyone?"

The Librarian smiled. "Yes."

CHAPTER THIRTY

San Marino, 1631

Antonius watched as Marinus and Paolo reached into their robes, produced identical keys, and unlocked multiple locks on the iron door in the deepest reaches of the Montale.

We must be inside Monte Titano.

Marinus had led them here, bypassing old cells and storage rooms along the way. Antonius hadn't realized the citadel contained a level this deep, but Marinus had guided them to the iron door unerringly and with unnerving haste. Old Paolo had remained silent and done his best to keep up.

Marinus turned the keys. A moment later, Antonius heard complicated mechanical devices release, followed by the door cracking open on its own, as if invisible hands pulled it. Antonius knew such clockworks existed, but they belonged in the courts and royal gardens of monarchs. His imagination would never have placed such a thing in the depths of Monte Titano.

Curiosity got the best of him. "What is this place?"

Marinus ignored him, but Paolo took pity on the youngster.

"This is where our greatest knowledge resides, Antonius. It houses the reason for the existence of our brotherhood."

That doesn't help. I want to know more!

Marinus hauled on the door, and unnatural green light bled into the tunnel from whatever lay beyond. Antonius recoiled but stopped when Paolo rested a reassuring hand on his shoulder.

"Steady, child. You were chosen to join our order because of your intellect and curiosity. Don't let fear betray the gifts God gave you."

Antonius swallowed his growing panic and stiffened his spine. Marinus motioned for him to follow and the young man complied, holding Paolo's hand as he entered the secret chamber.

As he stepped across the threshold, one hand trailing behind to lead Paolo inside, Antonius gawked.

The chamber was small but incredible. The walls curved around them, creating a round dome high above the impossibly smooth stone floor. The room was a marvel of architecture, which only served to enhance the unnatural feeling that permeated everything within it. If the room was a miracle, how was he to describe the stone table laden with books that floated at waist height in the room's center?

Antonius dropped Paolo's hand in shock. Sweat formed on the back of his neck, and his hands clutched his robes with a will of their own, pulling the fabric tightly around his body. Marinus had advanced into the room and stood on the opposite side of the table, staring at him. With a patient nod, he allowed Antonius to launch the barrage of questions his curiosity demanded he ask.

"What is this place, Marinus? Is this the work of God, or is it sorcery?"

"Are you certain those things are mutually exclusive, Antonius?"

The novitiate's eyes dropped to the floor. "I no longer know."

"When we recruited you, we believed you possessed a special mind. Your response just now proves we were correct in that assessment."

"Thank you, but…"

Marinus held up a hand. "You have many questions, as you should. I apologize, Antonius. I thought we had years to teach you what you need to know. To prepare you at a leisurely pace. However, events have overtaken our good intentions, and now I must ask you to trust us further. We have little time and must make our escape quickly."

As if to punctuate his point, the earth shook violently. Antonius' imagination conjured an image of the old pagan gods striking the mountain with a thunderbolt. He looked at the ceiling in shock.

Paolo shuffled forward. "Marinus, we have only moments to do what must be done. Gather the pieces of the *Codex* and be gone."

Marinus nodded and walked to a cabinet on the far side of the room. He returned with a pair of canvas packs, one of which bulged with supplies. He returned to the table, reverently picked up the leather-bound booklets one at a time, and placed them in the empty pack. After he finished, he looked at Antonius. "Come take this pack. It is time to leave." Shouts and musket fire echoed down the stairwell they had entered from. "Quickly, Antonius!"

Antonius shook himself and rushed forward. He took the proffered pack of supplies from Marinus while the monk shouldered the pack of books. The sound of booted feet clomping down stone stairs reached their ears.

Marinus turned and knelt at the far wall.

Antonius stared at him. *What is he doing? There's nothing there.*

The monk took a hunk of chalk from inside his robes and began drawing on the floor. Then he stood up and took a single step back. The sounds of their approaching attackers grew louder, and Antonius' blood pounded in his ears. A man's scream echoed, then abruptly ended. Antonius looked at Paolo for an explanation, but the old man was no longer facing him. Instead, he had moved to the doorway and stood staring blindly toward their approaching doom.

The novitiate turned frantically back to Marinus, only to experience another shock.

The monk stood with his eyes closed and his lips moving. The runes drawn in chalk at his feet glowed with a brighter version of the unnatural green light that lit the chamber. A section of the floor disappeared before Antonius' eyes as a stairwell materialized beneath the runes. The monk's eyes opened, and he turned his attention to the boy. "Come, Antonius."

Without another word, Marinus started down the stairs toward the green light that shone ahead of him.

Antonius wheeled back to Paolo, seeking comfort or explanation. The old man turned his vacant gaze on him. "Go, boy. Those steps lead to your salvation. Only hell awaits you here."

The novitiate gulped. "What about you, Brother Paolo?"

"My purpose is here. My time is coming to an end, but by permitting that, I allow yours to continue. Now, go!"

That command jolted Antonius into action. He hurried to the stairs and entered them. As his head cleared the floor, he heard a man's voice in the room above, cruel and strong, dripping contempt.

"Get out of the way, old man."

"Pandolfo, unless you have taken holy vows, you have no right to be here. Leave at once, and perhaps our Lord will forgive you this trespass."

A musket shot rang out, deafeningly close. Antonius heard Paolo grunt. The boy stopped in his tracks and turned to rush back up the stairs, but Marinus' strong hand grabbed him by the pack on his back, pulling him up short.

"Paolo knows what he's doing. What he has done. Do not waste his sacrifice!"

Antonius nodded amidst the green light. He turned to follow Marinus but heard Pandolfo's voice rise, first in anger and then in panic. "What are you doing? Stop! What in the name of—"

Pandolfo did not finish, and Antonius was flung down the

stairs atop Marinus as a blast of heat and flames consumed the chamber above him. When he regained his senses, the stairs had vanished, and the opening in the floor of the room above had become their ceiling. The green light that had guided him down the stairs had faded to a dim glow. Through the stone above his head, Antonius heard the muffled sounds of men screaming and sobbing in pain. Questions filled his head, but before he could give them voice, Marinus dragged him into deeper darkness.

CHAPTER THIRTY-ONE

Fairmount Park, Philadelphia

Watson left his Jeep in the darkened lot and walked calmly into the park with a shallow cardboard box tucked under his left arm. He zipped his jacket against the chill and the threat of rain. The sun had set, and the last light of the day was leaching from the world. The park closed at dusk, and as far as he could see, everyone else had left and he had it to himself.

Through the growing twilight, he approached the nearest of a quartet of concrete tables and benches, then hesitated as if he were unsure whether to choose this one or another. For a moment, he wondered if he'd made the right decision, coming alone without informing the authorities. He could well imagine Agent Colton's reaction when he found out. The mage cop would have filled the park with a score of fellow agents and a series of strategies and contingency plans to combat the lich.

That was the problem. Watson knew that if he could envision it, Malifa could as well, and it would prepare the necessary countermeasures. All too quickly, the whole thing would ratchet out of control. No, this was better. Simpler.

Watson selected the third of the four tables and took a seat on a bench facing the outer edge of the park. He set his box to one side and took a moment to run his fingers across the chessboard incised on the table's surface.

After opening the box, he carefully set up the pieces before speaking into the lonely night, infusing his voice with a drop of Will to make sure it was heard across the cables of magic. Aoede might not have been his or Malifa's strong suit, but every mage learned early how to listen for his own name. The classic "cocktail party" effect taught in every Psych 101 course applied to the perceptions of practitioners as well.

"You'll forgive the presumption, Iosefa, but I've taken white and will be going ahead with the first move." He studied the board for a moment more, then advanced a pawn.

Seconds ticked by with nothing but the sound of the breeze stirring dry leaves. Then, a shaft of light fell across the table from behind him as if a door had opened. It vanished just as quickly, and the skeletal form of Iosefa Malifa approached and rounded the table, then seated itself on the opposite bench.

"This is a lovely invitation, Derrick. I've missed our games."

"As much as I miss my old friend?"

The lich considered the board and made his move. "Perhaps, but I doubt it."

Dani, Stanley, and Trixie stood across the park, separated from the chess tables by a copse of trees.

Trixie huddled into her coat. "What is taking so long?"

"Be patient," Dani replied. "We have to trust Derrick."

"I do, I do. I'm worried about him. I do *not* trust Fat Mage."

A flash of light reached them through the trees. The trio straightened in anticipation. Stanley reached over and took both of Dani's hands.

"Are you ready for this? You haven't attempted any major

magic since you used the Codex fragment to summon your demon. Morphello is dangerous even in the most controlled conditions."

"Dammit, Stanley, we've been through this. Don't start second-guessing things now. It will be fine," she replied. "Just don't undermine my confidence. You're supposed to be helping me."

"The professor would never sanction this. It is certifiably crazy."

"Exactly, and because he'd never consider doing it, Malifa won't see it coming."

Trixie glanced at them, then resumed peering through the trees. "We're going to have to get a lot closer."

"Not a problem," replied Stanley. "Let's go over it again real quick. The spell is inscribed on the underside of their table. Once triggered, it will cycle three times before burning out. They'll loop through the same ninety-seven seconds each time, oblivious to the passage of time outside their immediate space. That's how long we'll have to close in and for you two to begin your spells."

Trixie raised an eyebrow. "I just realized there are four chess tables over there. How did you know which one to inscribe?"

"I didn't. I put the spell on each of them. Now, are we ready?"

Albert and H.H. huddled in front of Aron's hulking form on the far side of the park's restroom structure. The young mage tried not to gag, but every time the yeti shifted, it caused a new wave of body odor to waft up and outward as if magically propelled to assault nearby nostrils.

H.H. choked and covered its face with its front paws. "Come on, Aron! Your hygiene is giving demons a bad name."

"I just swam across an ocean last week. What more would you have me do, little imp?"

H.H. tilted its head up and down as if measuring the yeti. "I think we can get a crop-duster to fly over you and release fifty gallons of body spray. That might do the trick."

The yeti growled low in his throat, and H.H. wisely turned its attention back to the park.

Aron leaned closer, though out of necessity or spite, Albert couldn't say.

"Remember the plan," the yeti told him.

"I know. Something's been bugging me, though. If you can see through my illusions, won't Malifa be able to also?"

Aron shook his shaggy head, baring his fangs in what Albert hoped was a smile. "In life, he was a necromancer. A powerful one, but his power came through dedication and specialization. He is sensitive to the energies of life and their absence. He would detect an empty projection because it is lifeless, so we will not give him one. He cannot see through an illusion worn by a living body."

"Yeah, but still. Won't he—"

"You are letting what you think you know blind you to what you do not. My realm is intimately entwined with the flow of time, something you have not yet learned to weave into your illusions. When I look at your spells, I see through them, know them as false because they lack that dimension."

"But—"

The yeti silenced him with a threat of clamping a hand over the mage's mouth. "Do not worry about it, young one. If we survive this, I will show you how to add what you are lacking. Now, do you remember the plan?"

"We got it," insisted H.H.

"You had better. We will only get one chance."

Light flashed from across the park.

CHAPTER THIRTY-TWO

The Haven, Tuscany

"Let me get this straight." Storytime, as the Gliman had come to think of the Librarian's narrative, had come to an end. The same was true of the bottle of wine. "Your organization has existed for hundreds of years to respond to a prophecy that one day a mage will show up who goes from being a good guy to a bad guy."

"Crudely stated, but correct."

"After all those years of waiting, you think it's about to come true, and that Professor Derrick Watson is the guy?"

"He possesses a dangerous amount of power," explained the Librarian,

"So does Fat Mage. Hell, he has even more. Trust me; I've been on the receiving end of it more than once."

"It is not just raw power that concerns us. There have been more powerful practitioners than either of those men. Malifa, despite his accomplishments as a necromancer, is *only* a necromancer. Watson's talents are more diverse. That, coupled with his power and his change of state, suggests he is the Scorpion."

"Change of state? What does that mean? You're saying he

wasn't a candidate for fulfilling your prophecy until recently? What's changed?"

"He did."

"Come again?"

"For years, as he grew more skilled, Watson focused on being a scholar. Someone who researches the possibilities of demonic languages as opposed to someone who utilizes those skills in pursuit of specific outcomes."

"He's been in his ivory tower."

"Correct. That recently changed. Arguably, the actions of the necromancer were a precipitating factor."

"Me too," noted the Gliman.

"What? I don't understand."

"After Fat Mage kicked our asses the first time, back before he died and transformed himself, I confronted Watson."

"Confronted him how?"

"I got in his face about *not* using his power. I said all his learning was useless if he wasn't going to use it to achieve anything, like defeating Malifa."

The Librarian frowned. "How did he respond?"

The Gliman stared at her empty wine glass. "He grew a pair."

"Excuse me?"

"He manned up. Embraced his potential. He took out a small army of zombies, absorbing all the necromantic mojo that was animating them. I didn't even know that was possible. Then he went toe to toe with Malifa. The only reason he lost was that he put the well-being of his former students ahead of his own. That is why I don't think he's your Scorpion."

"Why?"

"You're looking for a bad guy. He isn't one."

"The same might once have been said about Iosefa Malifa."

The Gliman scowled. "You want me to become your new Curator, and what? My first task is to check up on Watson and make sure he's still a good guy and not turning into this Scorpion of yours?"

"Essentially."

"Huh. Okay, fine. Assuming this all still makes sense to me in the morning, challenge accepted!"

CHAPTER THIRTY-THREE

Fairmount Park, Philadelphia

"It's time," Stanley whispered before closing his eyes. He pushed his Will out through the trees and to the chess tables. "The spell is live. Let's move!"

The three mages took off at a jog. They didn't have far to go and didn't want to risk being seen too soon. It wasn't likely that Malifa had living allies in the area, but the undead were another matter.

Dani and Trixie skidded to a halt at the edge of the woods, using tree trunks to conceal themselves. Stanley stayed a few yards back, standing guard while the women prepared the next phase of their assault. He peered between the trees to glimpse Professor Watson. Unaware of his presence, Watson faced his way, meaning the lich had its back to them. Stanley knew he wasn't being rational, but it made the reptilian survival-focused part of his brain feel better that the big bad predator had its eyes pointing in another direction. Not that the skeleton possessed eyes.

Watson and Malifa appeared to be engrossed in their game. The professor's lips moved periodically, but Stanley had no idea what he was saying. It didn't matter. Dani and Trixie had prepared their spells in advance. In moments, Trixie's spell would begin to break down the outer layers of Malifa's bones, while Dani's spell would transmute them. They assumed the skeleton had magical protections, possibly even a broad-based defense drawing from Euskal, but any abjuration Malifa employed could only go so far when the bones required magic to animate them. The lich's defenses might weaken the spells Trixie and Dani had cast, but Stanley's skills would set up a time-loop, allowing the women to cast multiple times in a short span.

It looked like things are finally going according to plan.

Then the crazy wizard who had been all over the news stalked onto the scene from the parking lot behind Watson.

"You have got to be kidding me," Stanley whispered.

The lich considered the board and moved its first piece. "Perhaps, but I doubt it."

Watson experienced déjà vu but shrugged it off. It came again in meta-form, déjà vu of his déjà vu. Before he could reflect further, the world came rushing back at him, and he realized that both he and Malifa had been caught inside a temporal spell. Then the normal flow of time resumed, and he didn't have time to consider it further.

The mage who called himself Asombro stalked toward him through the night. Like everyone else, Watson had seen him on the news, but he hadn't realized how tall and imposing the man was. That impression was heightened by his black trench coat and flowing hair. Both billowed behind him as he approached.

The professor looked at the lich, about to scold him for using his invitation to create an ambush, but if a skeleton could look surprised, Malifa did. Its collar bones had shot up around its jaw, and it tilted its skull to one side in a posture that might have been astonishment or consternation or something else but was not recognition.

Asombro shouted at them across the lawn, his finger pointing behind them. "Malifa, behind you!"

Watson and Malifa spun sideways on their respective benches and were greeted by the full-throated, body-shaking bellow of Aron as the yeti charged across the lawn. Lich and mage jumped to their feet, each reaching for prepared spells. Before either could conjure, the yeti closed the distance with tremendous leaps and bounds. He landed next to Malifa with a crash that shook the park, swept a massive fist back, and prepared to strike the lich. The element of surprise had guaranteed he'd get in the first blow, and the yeti's size and strength would not require a second. The attack would end the battle moments after it had begun.

However, Asombro foiled Aron's plan.

Watson heard Asombro shout a hurried casting before he could release his own and watched, shocked, as the grass at the yeti's feet exploded. A gigantic hand of earth and stone shot up and wrapped around the yeti in an elemental grip. It pulled Aron away from Malifa and ruined his strike.

The earthen hand flung the yeti across the grass, but Aron was hardly finished. He tumbled, leapt back to his feet, and began swiping at the elemental creation, tearing away chunks with every swing. Watson backpedaled from the table, his eyes darting from one threat to the next.

Malifa regained its composure and turned to Watson. "A valiant try, Derrick. Truly. I didn't see this one coming. Either you've elevated your game, or you're as surprised as I am."

The lich flicked its hand and opened a portal. It turned to step through but paused. The green orbs in its skull flared, and Malifa looked down. Watson's eyes followed and saw what had given the lich pause. Its skeleton was flaking away. A flurry of dust surrounded it. Whole portions of bone were undergoing some kind of chemical reaction. They were bubbling, hissing, and sloughing off at an ever-increasing rate.

The lich looked at Watson. "Your alchemist puppy grows stronger, Derrick. I hadn't considered your lovesick girlfriend a threat and had intended to leave her out of all this, but now I realize I might have need of her services."

Invisible, Albert was shocked when he saw Malifa's skeleton start to shed, but he recognized the work as an alchemical reaction. When he scanned the park, it only took him a moment to spot Trixie and Dani. He sprinted to Trixie's side.

"Trixie! What the hell are you doing?"

She yelped in surprise. "Albert? Is that you?"

"Yes, of course it's me. Do you know another invisible guy with a Castilian accent? What are you doing here?"

"Me? What are *you* doing?" Trixie gasped through clenched teeth, still trying to transmute the calcium in Malifa's bones into potassium.

"I'm executing a plan to stop Malifa and help the professor."

"What plan? I didn't know of any plan. Well, besides *our* plan."

"It's the yeti's plan. Well, I guess it's mine too. The important thing is, it's not the professor's plan. The idea was to hit Malifa with a surprise attack."

Trixie nodded. "Oh, crap. That was our plan too. It *does* look surprised. Only... Uh-oh!"

Albert followed Trixie's gaze. The lich had turned to face them and unleashed a burst of green energy in their direction. The illusionist shoved Trixie down and leapt back, escaping the blast intended for her. The bolt tore into the tree she'd been using as cover, splintering the trunk but leaving them both unscathed.

Watson projected a blast of elemental fire at Malifa. The lich blocked it easily, reflexively calling up an anti-magic shield, but Watson had expected that. He doubted there was much he might do to injure the creature, but he *could* keep it distracted. He continued the barrage as he circled to the right, forcing the lich to focus on him and keep its shield in position.

Meanwhile, Aron had largely dismembered Asombro's creation and reoriented on the lich. The yeti pointed and yelled in his native tongue. Watson recognized it is a spell designed to slow down time against an individual.

Malifa was too fast or too prescient. The lich's shield flared with a burst of power that was more than sufficient to snuff out Watson's flames. It darted into the portal, which closed on its bony heels.

Watson spun, waiting for Malifa to reappear, but he wasn't the target. The yeti was. A new gate opened behind Aron, who had skidded to a halt when the lich disappeared.

"Aron, behind you!" Watson shouted, but he was too late. Malifa stepped out of the magical doorway and unleashed a torrent of necromantic energy into the unsuspecting yeti's hide.

Aron bellowed in rage and pain as purple light poured over him. He collapsed and writhed on the grass. Tongues of arcane fire licked his fur as he curled his massive body and sought to slow the flames of undead magic

Seconds later, a new earthen hand tore through the grass and wrapped around Aron, pinning him to the ground. Watson looked to his left and saw Asombro standing there, gloating about his imprisonment of the yeti.

Watson fumed, but he had to believe Aron could take care of himself. He returned his attention to Malifa, who, as he had hoped, was experiencing problems of its own.

The legs of the lich's skeleton had begun to transform. Its

femurs had stopped flaking off and were giving way to bark, starting to match the nearby trees. The new surface worked its way down its tibias and fibulas before Malifa blasted it with pulses of purple and black necromantic magic. The bark paused, and Malifa cackled.

"Oh, Derrick. You do have resourceful friends, and loyal too. If only you had shown me the same degree of engagement."

"I did, Iosefa. I always did."

"Never! You looked down on me, Derrick. Admit it!"

"That's not true!" Watson shouted as his brain scrambled for a plan of action.

It didn't matter. Malifa fed more power into its spell, and its skeletal legs began to re-form, enchanted obsidian bone replacing the plant matter barely faster than it was being transformed. Then the lich spun at the waist and hurled green and purple lightning bolts into the nearby trees.

Watson heard Dani scream and abandoned any complex tactics. He lashed out with his Will, and with the most basic of spells, ripped one of the concrete tables out of the ground, spinning it end over end to collide with the lich.

The force of the blow sent Malifa flying. It crashed into the ground but regained its feet almost immediately. "You can't defeat me like...ack!" Malifa screamed as another table crashed into it head-on, flattening it against the ground five feet from where it'd been standing.

Seconds later, the table flew to the side, propelled by a blast of the lich's magic. Watson launched a third concrete missile at it, but Malifa was not taken off-guard again. The table shattered against its shield.

Watson moved to fling the fourth table in a desperate attempt to buy his friends more time, but Malifa smacked him with a blast of kinetic force before he could act, knocking the professor on his ass.

Watson rolled to his left and got to his knees, gasping for

breath. He had to fight back. He had to help his friends. Their magic could not compete with the combined effects of Malifa and the new mage Asombro, with whom it had somehow formed an alliance.

Aron's efforts had been neutralized almost as quickly as they had begun. Worst of all, whatever element of surprise Dani and Trixie had possessed was now gone. It was just a matter of time before the lich regrouped and picked them off.

The professor got to his feet and turned back to the lich, grunting with the pain of two or three bruised ribs. Malifa had dismissed him from its awareness and focused on fighting the transmutational magic that still threatened to destroy its body. Watson wasn't sure what effect it would have on the lich, but Malifa was clearly concerned.

The lich slashed its hand through the air and ripped open another portal. Seconds later, zombies poured forth, alert to their master's command. "There are mages in the trees. Attack them!" Like a squad of undead enforcers, they shuffled off to do their jobs, freeing Malifa to focus its full attention on pushing back the effects of Dani's magic. Watson decided to make it harder.

Using his Will like a lasso, he flung the remaining chess table at Malifa. The result was the same, causing little more than an annoyance to the lich, but he followed it up with a renewed conflagration. Watson channeled Will into the flames, pouring them on as he advanced on Malifa. He knew the lich was more powerful, but he dared hope that the large number of threats would make a difference.

It almost did. Malifa growled in frustration, but before Dani and Trixie's magic could cause more damage, it opened another of its damnable portals, flung itself through, and closed it as soon as it was clear.

"Shit! I lost him," Dani cursed from the trees.

For a moment, everything was quiet. The zombies had all but reached their quarry, but they paused, then fell limply to the ground, cut off from the lich and its animating magic. Watson let out a deep breath and looked around to take stock of the situation.

Dani, Trixie, and Stanley emerged from the tree line. Their eyes were locked on Asombro, who was slowly backing away from the group. Aron remained down, imprisoned by the mage's elemental fist.

Then a new portal opened, and Malifa stepped back into the world with another figure at its side. Watson didn't know the young man, but he recognized that Malifa's magic held the man in thrall. The lich had taken control of a new victim, doubtless another mage, and could now command its puppet's spells as well as its own.

"Oh, crap," the professor muttered.

Malifa waved its phalanges in Watson's direction and spoke to its companion. "Deal with him."

Instinctively, Watson threw up a shield, but the mage didn't hit him from the front with anything like Malifa's blasts of lightning. Instead, gale-force winds slammed into his spine like an all-pro linebacker. Watson bounced off the ground face-first. Blood flowed from his nose, and he was left gasping for breath as his bruised ribs cracked. Then the winds shifted and pressed down on him from above, making the simple act of breathing still more difficult and further maneuvers impossible.

As he struggled, Watson caught a flash of movement to his right. It was Albert. Enraged, his assistant charged toward Asombro with an aluminum baseball bat clutched in his hands.

That was not going to work.

Asombro detected the new threat. He spun and unleashed a spell. The ground buckled under Albert's feet, sending the young mage crashing down. In the next instant, the earth rose and covered Albert's hands and feet, pinning him in place. He struggled, but it was a futile effort.

A moment later, the zombies animated again and resumed

their previous course. In seconds, they overwhelmed and captured Watson's closest friends. Stanley, Dani, and Trixie all emerged from the trees, clutched by undead and unyielding hands. They were bruised and beaten. Worse, they looked exhausted, their magic and Will depleted. Any lingering strength they'd had left, they'd spent fighting the zombies.

Through the bruises, Trixie flashed him a big blood-stained smile.

Watson responded on a primal level, feeling pride and attraction for the woman he loved no matter that they had just lost. That only lasted for an instant. He pushed all thoughts of his girlfriend out of his mind and took stock. Aron and Albert were pinned by earth elementals, courtesy of Asombro. Trixie and two of his former students were held by zombies. Malifa's new thrall, a rare Dushara-speaker, had him hopelessly pinned.

It totally sucked.

A pair of skeletal feet stopped in front of Watson's face, blocking his view. The wind let up just enough that he could crane his neck to gaze at Malifa's hideous skull and stare into the glowing green pits of its eye sockets. The lich knelt to bring its visage closer.

"I have to hand it to you, Derrick. You were magnificent. Truly. You have never played the game so well. So…unexpectedly. You did what so many humans can't even conceive of, let alone achieve. You ignored your nature. You went against all your instincts. It *almost* worked."

The lich rose and swept its arm out, encompassing Watson's beloved friends. "You have impressive comrades, too. More impressive than I realized. That speaks highly for you."

Malifa stalked toward Stanley. "Yes, the FBI agent who can bend time. I should have seen that little trick coming." It moved on and traced the bones of its index finger down Dani's cheek. She spat on it.

"My first pet. The transmogrificationist and humanitarian. So much power, so little direction or ambition. It really is a shame." Malifa continued its cocky jaunt and stopped in front of Trixie, who glared daggers at him. The lich turned its skull back toward Watson. "Out of respect for our friendship, I will only say that this young lady is remarkable. To have her alchemical acumen at such a young age is special. I do hope you appreciate her."

"She's amazing. She's also none of your damn business," Watson growled.

The lich shrugged its collar bones and continued its tour, stopping next to Asombro. Malifa pointed at the captive yeti. "And you! You are damn impressive. How long have you been on Earth? Such incredible power. I only wish my magic worked on non-humans. Oh, the things we could accomplish..." Its voice trailed off wistfully.

It turned to Albert and placed its phalanges on its pelvic bones in a mockery of a man standing with arms akimbo. "Last *and* most certainly least, the boy with no Will. I pity you. You're a prisoner of your own mind and society's ridiculous notions of normality. I wonder how differently you might have turned out if you'd been my pupil."

Malifa leaned down to pat Albert's head condescendingly, only to pause. It jerked upright and looked at the gathered mages.

"You aren't real!"

Albert looked up at him and grinned. Then a voice—Albert's voice—came out of nowhere.

"Well, damn. Aron, you were right."

Malifa spun around but found nothing to see.

"Is this an illusion? Impossible. You're Derrick's broken prodigy. The boy with all the knowledge but no power."

"Oh, he has power," assured Asombro. "More than enough to topple most human mages."

Malifa spun again, its skull turning back and forth as if comparing Albert and Asombro. "I see. Family resemblance, is it? You've apparently come into power but without the requisite self-esteem. This is a complicated masquerade, though ultimately a useless one." The necromancer snapped its fingers, and Oleg obliged with an incredible wind that drove Asombro to his knees in front of Malifa. "I'll deal with you soon. I might have use for you after all."

Nearby, Aron howled and shook against his bonds. Malifa turned to consider him anew. "You are the unexpected piece on the board." He paused. "Such savagery and such a horrible appearance. I also suspect I should be grateful that my mortal ability to smell no longer bothers me. I'd always believed native speakers of Hægt to be deep thinkers. Long-term strategists, not brutish."

The yeti stared back. Watson wished he could hear what Aron was thinking.

Then Asombro spoke.

"Oh, we are," the mage insisted, rising to his feet despite the punishing winds. "It's because we take our time with any task. We consider your game of chess a pastime for young children. Thank you for getting close enough for me to demonstrate this for you firsthand." Time slowed for everything and everyone except Asombro. The image of the elementalist shifted and grew into the yeti, and Aron closed its massive hairy hands on the necromancer's skeleton. It tore it apart one joint after another with incredible savagery.

Explosions of necromantic magic erupted as the lich struggled in the yeti's grip, but it was futile. Too slow to accomplish anything, wrapped as it was in thick layers of compressed time. The last vestiges of Albert's illusion of Asombro fell away, and Watson watched in awe as the yeti proceeded to shatter Malifa's bones, ignoring the damage he suffered as he ripped the lich's magical skeleton apart.

Aron had time on his side. Each wound Malifa inflicted on the yeti, injuries that would have stopped a human, was healed before the next occurred, as months passed with each second. In the end, Aron had plenty of spare moments to snap and crush every last one of Malifa's bones multiple times.

Finally, apparently satisfied, Aron tossed the last fragments of the lich on the ground, and the normal flow of time resumed. The fist of earth that had held him prisoner faded. The prison holding Albert disappeared as well, leaving behind a grinning hamster who darted between the Dushara-speaker's legs.

Finally, Albert—the real Albert—became visible. He stood behind Oleg with a real baseball bat clutched in his hands. He hit the man on the shoulder, and the suborned mage crumpled to the ground. His spell dissipated, and Watson was free.

The professor struggled to his feet, clutching his side and taking ragged, grateful breaths. He surveyed his friends.

The zombies had collapsed again, freed of animation and motivation by Malifa's defeat. His friends stepped away from the corpses.

Albert knelt to check the unconscious mage's pulse before looking up and offering them a thumbs-up. H.H. scampered up to Watson's feet with a cheesy grin plastered across its furry face.

"Bet you didn't see *that* coming, huh, big guy?"

CHAPTER THIRTY-FOUR

Alexander University, Philadelphia
"Alberto Hernandez Alcaldo!"

Albert straightened his gown and strode onto the stage. The glare of the auditorium's lights was matched by the gleam of his self-assured smile as he approached the university's president and shook the woman's hand.

Watson wore an equally broad grin as he approached from the opposite direction. He looked into Albert's eyes and nodded. "Congratulations, Doctor." He draped a black hood lined with white and purple silk across Albert's shoulders.

Everyone crowded into Watson's office to celebrate Albert's graduation. Trixie had arranged a selection of food from Albert's favorite tapas restaurant, as well as more bottles of champagne than they'd be able to drink, though everyone did their best. As a result, they were all in a joyous mood when Watson knocked his fist on the desk to get their attention before turning to face his protégé.

"I couldn't be prouder of you if you were my son, Albert. You've worked long and hard for this moment."

"Too hard, if you ask me," boomed H.H. from its perch in a fold of Albert's doctoral hood before going back to chewing on the gold tassel dangling from his tam.

"What are you going to do now?" asked Trixie.

"Honestly? I haven't given it much thought," admitted Albert. "It feels like I've been a student forever, all theory and no application."

"I think it's safe to say you've graduated from pure theory," Stanley offered. He opened a fresh bottle of champagne and made the rounds to refill everyone's glass.

"There's still a lot of work to do, repairing the damage Malifa did," noted Watson. "I'd welcome your help."

Albert flushed. "Don't take this the wrong way, Professor, but I think I need to take a break from being your student."

"I couldn't agree more. You're done with that. I wasn't suggesting you work for me."

"Then what?"

"I thought we might work together as colleagues and equals. Clearly, there are more than a few things you can teach me."

AUTHORS' NOTE

WRITTEN MAY 9, 2022

Hey, you're back! Not that we're surprised, mind you. We really like these characters and never doubted that you would too, but it's hard for authors to be objective about their work. So, thank you very much for reading *At the Speed of Yeti* and reassuring us that you're enjoying the unfolding story of our professor of demonic languages.

The keyword is "unfolding." There's a lot in this book that you probably never expected you'd find after reading book one, not least of which was the yeti we teased you with from the start with the title. We think it's fair to say you'll find still more surprises in the next book, *Undead Alternatives*, because that's how we roll: a balanced blend of things-readers-can-predict/hope-for based on the worldbuilding we've already done and story arcs already hinted at and never-saw-that-coming pieces as we reveal more of the universe to you.

Along the way, earlier characters will grow and change, minor characters can take on significance and agency, and you can expect new characters to emerge in unexpected ways. Why are we doing this? Lots of reasons, but here are three:

AUTHORS' NOTE

1) We want to keep you entertained. That's our job. That's why you came here.

2) Keeping you entertained isn't enough. It's a good place to start, but we don't want you to grow complacent, so we will continue to raise the bar, challenge your expectations, and, oh, yeah, keep you entertained (see that first point).

3) We like challenging ourselves too. Long before either of us became writers, we were readers. We know the feeling of getting lost in a book. In particular, we grew up reading both stand-alone novels and series, but a strong case can be made that it was the series that set us on the road to being the writers we became. That experience of reading book after book of continuing characters and ever more familiar venues.

Novels that did that for us created a feeling of coming home and the certainty that a familiar comfort could be found within the pages of each successive volume. So maybe a fourth reason (we said there were lots of them) for why we're writing these books is that we're repaying (or paying forward) the gifts we received from other writers in years past.

With that in mind, we thought you might like to know who some of the authors who shaped us were.

Like so many of his generation of readers who would go on to write science fiction and fantasy, Lawrence cut his teeth on Heinlein's juveniles, books like *Space Cadet* and *Have Space Suit— Will Travel*. Basically, boys' adventure books that suggested anything was possible. Alongside these, he immersed himself in the multi-volume story arcs of Edger Rice Burroughs, traveling to Mars and Venus and deep into the Earth's inner core (as well as occasional trips to the jungles of Africa). Decades later, Lawrence picked up *A Princess of Mars* to revisit the wonder and delight of his youth, but the experience wasn't quite the same. Or, as he remarked to his wife, "Somewhere in the intervening years, someone snuck in and rewrote these books, adding in buckets of racism and sexism. WTF?"

AUTHORS' NOTE

As he progressed through his teens, Lawrence was influenced and shaped by fresh ideas and perspectives of New Wave authors like Ursula K. Le Guin and Roger Zelazny, writers who introduced concepts from anthropology, psychology, and other social sciences into their fiction. They opened him up to new possibilities and ways of thinking, not just about the fiction he was reading but the world around him as well. Whether sailing a tiny boat amidst the Earthsea archipelagos or walking through Shadow to stand upon the cliffs and gaze down at the Courts of Chaos, he was forever changed. There was no going back, and going forward ultimately meant writing his own books.

Brian, for his part, was shaped by the work of Margaret Weis and Tracy Hickman. They were the co-authors of the original *Drangonlance* novels he has read and reread many times. They provided a depth of adventure and fantasy that has stayed fresh and inspiring after all these years, and he remains an avid follower of their work. Not surprisingly, Brian found his way to R.A. Salvatore, Troy Denning, Paul S. Kemp, and other RPG-related authors in his teens to satisfy a constant thirst for fantasy and adventure. Later, while serving in Iraq, Brian was introduced to *Harry Potter* and the joy of YA literature and worldbuilding.

Suffice it to say, Brian's appetites haven't slowed down any. Recently he has devoured djinn brought to life by P. Djeli Clark and plumbed the grim depths of Joe Abercrombie's dark universe.

Given where we're coming from, you could make either of two arguments: that it seems impossible the two of us could ever come together to write our novels, or that our collaboration was inevitable and it was just a matter of time before destiny threw us together.

That's the great thing about having people of different backgrounds and experiences: we challenge one another, we surprise one another, and we argue about what works (and doesn't work) in a story because we're coming at it from different places, and the process of resolving those issues results in a better book. It keeps us from becoming too predictable, much like the lesson Watson learns in the course of this book (c'mon, you knew we'd bring it back to the book, right?). Readers, like maniacal necromancers, have to be kept on their toes.

The trick, both for us and our characters, is now that we've come up with the unexpected, we're going to have to keep raising that bar. We're okay with that since we like the challenge and we feel that obligation to the characters we've created. Okay, sure, it doesn't hurt that we've already written the third book, so we know that we've already met that goal. For now, you'll have to take our word for it, but not for long. Book three, *Undead Alternatives*, is just a month away.

In the meantime, we hope you'll share some feedback with us about this book by posting reviews, talking it up on social media, and letting us know what your favorite scene or character was. Seriously, we don't want to become complacent either.

ACKNOWLEDGMENTS

As always, we must begin by thanking our partners for their love and support. It can't be easy living with crazy men who talk to themselves and engage in imaginary dialogues with their fictional characters. They do it, and without them in our lives, the books of *the Demon Codex* wouldn't come to life.

Next in line, we would be utter cads not to acknowledge the backing of our extended family and friends. Be they children, fellow writers, or just people that listen to us complain, though they are too numerous to name, please know you very much helped make this all possible.

Finally, we happily thank the team at LMBPN. Their steadfast belief in our work, in our potential, kept us on task. This series marks a launching point for us as a team, and the future looks bright indeed. The support and savvy of Michael, Judith, Robin, Lynne, Kelly, Steve, and the many others at LMBPN make it possible for us to focus on storytelling while they make sure our words find their way into the hands of our favorite people, the readers.

ABOUT BRIAN THORNE

Brian Thorne is a former Marine and intelligence officer. These days, he works in cybersecurity when he's not playing chauffeur to his son or training his new rescue dog. Additionally, he and his beautiful partner are avid travelers, which provides much fodder for writing...oh yeah...writing. He also writes, when he has time.

Brian believes that we all need to slow down and spend more time asking how we can help each other. He advocates for at-risk veterans and those that need a hand. He loves building houses for those in need and sharing his not-so-subtle opinions with legislators when they'll listen.

A recent transplant to Texas, has undertaken a noble quest to find the perfect brisket and share news of it with the world. He views it as his crowning contribution to humanity.

Newsletter Link:

To follow Brian on his writing adventure, keep up to date on his brisket quest, and receive a free short story, you can join his newsletter at http://bit.ly/ThorneNews. Your email address will not be sold, rented, or in any other way disseminated.

ABOUT LAWRENCE M. SCHOEN

Lawrence M. Schoen holds a Ph.D. in cognitive psychology and psycholinguistics. He spent ten years as a college professor, doing research in the areas of human memory and language. This was followed by seventeen years as the director of research for a medical center in Philadelphia that provided mental health and addiction services.

He's also the founder of the Klingon Language Institute, and since 1992, he has championed the exploration and use of this constructed tongue throughout the world. In addition, he occasionally works as a hypnotherapist specializing in authors' issues. And too, he is a cancer survivor.

In 2007, he was a finalist for the Astounding Award for Best New Writer. He received a Hugo Award nomination for Best Short Story in 2010 and Nebula Award nominations for Best Novella in 2013, 2014, 2015, and 2018, for Best Novelette in 2019, and for Best Novel in 2016.

Some of his most popular writing deals with the ongoing humorous adventures of a spacefaring stage hypnotist named the Amazing Conroy and his companion animal Reggie, an alien buffalito that can eat anything and farts oxygen.

ABOUT LAWRENCE M. SCHOEN

His *Barsk* series represents his more serious work and uses anthropomorphic SF to explore ideas of prophecy, intolerance, political betrayal, speaking to the dead, predestination, and free will. It's also earned him the Cóyotl Award for Best Novel of 2015 and again in 2018.

Lawrence lives near Philadelphia with his wife Valerie, who is neither a psychologist nor a Klingon-speaker.

Newsletter Link:

If you would like updates on Lawrence's new releases, appearances, or special offers, please consider joining his mailing list. Your email address will not be sold, rented, or in any other way disseminated. Simply use this link to sign up: http://bit.ly/LMS-join

ALSO BY LAWRENCE M. SCHOEN

Barsk

Barsk: The Elephants' Graveyard

(2015 Nebula Award Finalist, 2015 Winner Cóyotl Award)

The Moons of Barsk

(2018 Winner Cóyotl Award)

Excerpts of Jorl ben Tral

Soup of the Moment

Pizlo's Limits

SERIES IN THE "CONROYVERSE"

Conroyverse: A Sampler

("Buffalo Dogs," *Buffalito Destiny, Ace of Corpses,* and *Slice of Entropy*)

The Amazing Conroy

Buffalito Bundle

(includes "Yesterday's Taste," 2011 WSFA Small Press Award Finalist)

Barry's Tale

(2012 Nebula Award Finalist)

Calendrical Regression

(2014 Nebula Award Finalist)

Barry's Deal

(2017 Nebula Award Finalist)

Buffalito Destiny

Trial of the Century

(2013 Nebula Award Finalist)

Buffalito Contingency

Command Performance

(The Amazing Conroy Omnibus Edition)

Freelance Courier

Ace of Corpses

Ace of Saints

Ace of Thralls

Ace of Agency

(Freelance Courier Books 1 - 3)

Pizza In Space

Slice of Entropy

Slice of Chaos

Pirates of Sol

Pirates of Marz

Seeds of War (with Jonathan Brazee)

Invasion

Scorched Earth

Bitter Harvest

Seeds of War Trilogy

Adrenaline Rush (with Brian Thorne)

Fight or Flight

Alien Thrill Seeker

Anger Management

Adrenaline Rush

The Demon Codex (with Brian Thorne)

Soul Bottles

At The Speed Of Yeti

Undead Alternatives

Collections

Creature Academy:

Cautionary Poems of Public Education

Sweet Potato Pie and other stories

The Rule of Three and other stories

Openings without Closure

Transcendent Boston and other stories

Non-Fiction

Eating Authors: One Hundred Writers'
Most Memorable Meals

Author Website:

http://www.lawrencemschoen.com/books/

OTHER BOOKS FROM LMBPN PUBLISHING

Sign up for the LMBPN email list to be notified of new releases and special deals!

https://lmbpn.com/email/

For a complete list of books by LMBPN please visit:

https://lmbpn.com/books-by-lmbpn-publishing/

www.ingramcontent.com/pod-product-compliance
Lightning Source LLC
LaVergne TN
LVHW041928070526
838199LV00051BA/2748